Duet Showers

KESHAV PATHAK

BlueRose ONE
Stories Matter
New Delhi • London

BLUEROSE PUBLISHERS
India | U.K.

For permissions requests or inquiries regarding this publication, please contact:

BLUEROSE PUBLISHERS
www.BlueRoseONE.com
info@bluerosepublishers.com
+91 8882 898 898
+4407342408967

ISBN: 978-93-6783-380-3

Cover Design: Aman Sharma
Typesetting: Pooja Sharma

First Edition: January 2025

You find love when you least expect it,

And lose it when you are sure it is in your grasp.

Ruskin Bond

About the Author

Keshav Pathak was born and raised in a town named Kekri located near Ajmer in Rajasthan. He is a 25-year old graduate student from RIE Ajmer. Being a biology student, he was one of the many students to go to Kota to study for the medical and engineering exams. Kota left an impression on him after his time there. He's currently purusing his higher studies in Ajmer itself. Despite being a science student, his hobbies include reading, writing, singing, poetry, a little sketching and sometimes calligraphy. 'Duet Showers' is his first book.

Backstory

Kota. The educational hub of India. People from all the states and localities come to Kota for study of competition exams like NEET, JEE, etc. When Mr V.K. Bansal established the first coaching institute 'Bansal classes' in 1985, it sowed the seed for the subsequent development of 'coaching industry' in Kota. As the inflow of aspirants increased, so did the number of coaching institutes. This also led for business opportunities for the public of Kota. People started to rent out rooms to students and some started mess and catering services. In Kota, anyone can find houses with a to-let sign on the front. Some signs also list priorities like 'for girls' or 'for boys'. The soon-to-be-metropolitan city is divided into various sectors like Mahavir Nagar, Dadabari, Nayapura, etc.

In the Mahavir Nagar-1st, there exists a hostel which is the ultimate telly talk of the neighbourhood. Apart from this hostel being the most facilitated and having more than 10 floors, its back-story makes this hostel more famous.

This hostel is result of the minds of two twin sisters, Aarti and Aaradhna. After spending their childhood and most of the teenage in dream city Mumbai, they both decided to have a business of their own just like their father. They decided to open a chain of hostels in different parts of the country. Since they had an uninhabited property in Kota, they decided to open their first hostel there. After all, what better place can there be than the education hub Kota to start a hostel? Firstly, they took their father's permission for building a hostel on that property. Then they tore down the house that was built on that property. Then they built a hostel of a great height with great facilities and with the collaboration with a good mess. With apartment like rooms, A & A hostel was ready. A great inauguration party was held and many people of different states with high positions were invited. Of course with facilities like theirs, the charge per room was high; but still they found people attracted towards their hostel. People found the price reasonable for such great rooms. With a kick-start, their business was ready to spread its wings in the sky of market. The first three years of this hostel was the golden period.

After that, one day both sisters were infected by an illness with no cure— also called as love. Both of the sisters fell in love with the same man. The man was supposed to be a sponsor for their future hostel building. Even though they both agreed this was unprofessional, but who has been able to make heart agree with anything? It began all sweet and sheepish as they both realised that they were in love with the same man, but soon— allegedly—they both started to plot against each other to win that man's love.

The plotting ultimately resulted—as it does most of the times—in no one getting the man. Then both of them found out—allegedly—that their sister was evil-plotting against them. As the neighbourhood people tell, there were many arguments for many days and even nights. One day, they got the news of their father dying in a car accident. After the distribution of rest of the property amongst them, both wanted the hostel for themselves. After a long and heated legal fight, it was decided that the property would be divided equally and so the hostel was divided into two, joined by a wall. The long corridors turned into two half-long corridors. The main nameplate was taken down and both the hostels were named as 'A & A girls' hostel' and 'A & A boys' hostel'. Both sisters now live in their respective hostels and do the job of warden. The mornings and evenings are times of entertainment for the neighbours as both sisters argue over small, insignificant things just to insult one another.

The End.

El Fin.

Das Ende.

But wait… haven't you heard?

One story's graveyard is another story's garden.

And this is where another story begins.

I

At third floor of the A & A boys' hostel—inside room no. 305—the boy was putting on his black colour jacket over his black shirt. He was preparing for the birthday party of his best friend. He fixed his hairstyle up a little bit by using gel. Then he reached out for his black tie hanging on the hangar right beside the mirror. He wore his tie, set his black pants a little and took a good look at himself. His hair were perfectly coiffed, his face was glowing because of recently used face-wash, he had his sideburns trimmed and had a light stubble. His body looked athletic in the suit and his plain-toed, black oxford shoes only accentuated his charisma. As a final touch, he sprayed some perfume under his armpits, on both sides of his neck and on his wrists. He was ready to have some fun at the party.

At third floor of the A & A girls' hostel—inside room no. 306—the girl was having some difficulty putting her jeans on. The navy blue jeans were tight around her thighs. After putting one leg through, she bounced on that leg while trying to put the other one in. After trying two times, she lay down on the bed and started to put her other leg in. Then she stood up and did little jumps while pulling the jeans up. She did the button and pulled the chain up. She put on her black top and started to do her hair. First, she thought to make a bun, started and then rejected the idea. Then she thought to go with the messy hairstyle that was in fashion, started, but then rejected the idea because it was taking too much time. Finally, she settled on open hair and then she looked at herself. Her tight jeans made the space between her legs bigger and hugged her butt tight, making it to pop out. The top was okay with the fitting and it also made her breasts to pop out, making her belly look more flat. She ran her fingers through her hair sometimes and adjusted her hair. She was a bit uncomfortable with her jeans but she knew that her boyfriend liked her butt. She was ready to draw her boyfriend's attention at the party, along with many others.

II

The party was in a marriage garden. The marriage garden was south of the hostel which included a labyrinth of streets. There was one landmark about that garden. That garden was situated diagonally to a government school. There were average decorations in the garden, but on top of the entrance gate, there were large, glitter-decorated letters which spelled, 'HAPPY BIRTHDAY CHANDA AND CHAYANSH' in two neatly spaced rows. There was food as well, kit up in a buffet. There were waiters roaming around serving people with flavoured potato nuggets as a light snack.

All of Chayansh's friends were there except one. He was late as usual but they didn't care. He was always late, even in class. They had their eyes fixed on the entry gate—imagining him to come running in, sweating all over his creased clothes. He would run straight towards their group and start giving excuses while catching his breath. Suddenly they saw him coming in; no running, no sweat, just calm and stylish walking. He was in all-black attire. He was wearing black jacket along with black shirt and pants and even his tie was black. For the first time, they saw his hairs were perfectly coiffed and he looked more handsome than them or possibly anyone at the party.

He slowly walked up to them. The group noticed that he got some glances and second glances by some girls on his way, if he didn't notice. He stood in front of them, turned a full circle and asked, "So, how do I look?"

"Where are your manners, man?" one of his friends said.

"Sorry. Happy birthday, bro." He forwarded his hand.

"Thanks, Shantu." Chayansh replied shaking his hand.

"So, how do I look?"

"Well, Mr. Shantanu Sharma, you're making me question my sexuality."

"I can't decide whether it's a compliment or not."

"It's a compliment, dude. The bottom line is; I am impressed."

"Wow. The fastidious Chayansh is impressed. I feel honoured. It was a real pleasure impressing you."

"From the circumstances, it looks like you've impressed more people other than Chayansh." Chayansh's sister Chanda said barging into the group.

Chanda and Chayansh were twins. Both of them were named according to their parents. Their mom's name was Chaaya and Chayansh was named with respect to her name. Their father's name was Chandrashekhar from which Chanda's name was given.

Chanda was born a sweet and disciplined child like her father who grew up to be a smart, attractive and disciplined-only-in-front-of-elders type 17 year old late bloomer. She had her first period 6 days ago and she could still feel the pain a little. Nobody knew that except her mother and father. They had told her that it was okay if she didn't want to come to the party but she insisted. She really wanted to go. Partly because it was her birthday as well and partly because she knew that Shantanu would come to the party.

"Happy birthday, Chanda." Shantanu forwarded his hand in the present.

"Thanks, Shantu." Chanda shook his hand. She felt Goosebumps and electricity running through her body like she always did at his touch.

She had first met him when she was in 8th class. He had come to their home for group studying. In their group there were four people that day; Shantanu, her brother Chayansh, her friend Sonia and herself. The day went by completely normal but before sleeping that night, she was wondering why she felt electricity when Shantanu's hand suddenly brushed against hers. She started thinking about him more and more as time passed and the question of Goosebumps and electricity remained unanswered. Soon, as fate would have it, she started to like him. But she never said it.

Unlike the regular case, she never let anybody get a hint that she was into him except Shantanu. He seemed to have a hint about her feelings but she felt that he brushed them off because she was his friend's sister. But that never stopped her from trying to flirt with him.

"Ansh, mom has called for you and your friends were called by their parents as well." Chanda said to Chayansh, who was known as Ansh to every family member. Everyone left except Shantanu and her, since his parents weren't at the party.

"Wow. You're looking like a real ladies man today. If I might add, you're looking sexy after a very long time." She said checking him out.

"Well, thank you very much. It means so much coming from a girl. You too look good."

"Only good...?"

"Well, you do seem a little weak. It's as if you've had some kind of disease."

"It probably would've been better if it was a disease."

"Why? What happened?"

She smiled internally at his genuine worried look.

"Well, if you must know, I had my menarche 5-6 days ago."

"That's great."

"What? It's not great."

"I know it pains but that's part and parcel of the process."

"You don't know about it. You *won't* know about it. It transcends the definition of pain."

"You know, next time you can hold my hand when it pains. I'm told to radiate great amounts of positive energy which is good for pain." Shantanu joked.

Chanda stood beside him and held his hand gently, again feeling the Goosebumps and the electricity. He felt a mixed feeling. It had the mixture of happiness of a girl flirting with him, shyness from her touch and the guilt of flirting with his friend's sister. He still didn't know why he feels guilt in that. It's not him that's flirting, but still it feels as if he's doing something forbidden. She was still holding his hand.

"Is this okay or should I hold it more *firmly*?" She tightened her grip.

"Listen, don't take this too seriously. I was just joking." He said freeing his hand uncomfortably.

Shantanu's reaction was exactly what Chanda had expected, but still she felt embarrassed and humiliated. It wasn't something new but it always hurt the same if not more. She kept her composure and said chuckling, "So was I." They both laughed on her 'supposed humour'.

"You're a good actress. For a moment, I thought..."

"What?" She asked with hope.

He only shrugged.

"What? What did you think was going to happen, you idiot?"

Suddenly she heard her mom calling her. She excused herself and walked over to her mom. On the way, she was asking herself the same question she asked Shantanu.

What? What did you think was going to happen, you idiot?

III

Chanda walked up to her mom and asked her what she wanted. Beside her, standing was Chanda's best friend. She was wearing black top and navy blue jeans. She looked surprisingly good in such a simple style. Chaaya said that she was looking for her so she called her here. Chanda walked up to her and said, "You know, Poorna, it's usually other people who come to the birthday girl, not the other way around."

"Well then, I guess I'm *other people* now, huh?"

"Oh, you're always my darling and you know that."

Chanda and Poorna hugged and she wished her happy birthday. Chaaya got busy with the baker. She told them that there was going to be a delay in delivery of cake as there was an accident on the way to here and the traffic was diverted. Poorna took a good look at Chanda. She was wearing black jeans along with a dark blue top which also had a jacket like addition sewed at the shoulders of the top inside. If it weren't for her weak and ashen face, she would've looked far better than her.

"You look good." Poorna said with hesitation.

"Only good...?"

"I mean, your face looks a bit weak. Did you have a disease recently?"

"No."

"Then what is it?"

"As my best friend, I'm telling you this. I had my menarche around 5-6 days ago."

"You had your... what? Speak a language other than biology."

"...My first period." She said with a sigh.

"Wow. That's splendid."

"Why does everyone thinks that it is a good thing? It feels like someone has stabbed my lower abdomen and is twisting the knife all the time."

"Calm down; here," she grabbed a nugget from a nearby waiter's plate and handed it to her, "have a nugget."

Chanda gobbled up the nugget and then told the waiter to leave the plate with her. The waiter obeyed and then she asked Poorna for remedies for this pain.

After sometime discussing remedies and other topics, the cake arrived. The cake was extraordinary. Nobody had seen that big and stylish cake. The height of the cake was around 4 feet and it was being brought on a stool with a circular seat with wheels on the legs. The cake was placed in the centre of the garden and everyone gathered around the cake in a semicircle. Chanda and Chayansh came forward and tried to blow all the candles on the cake but failed, so they spent a few minutes blowing the remaining candles. Then they cut the cake while everyone sang 'happy birthday' in unison. They fed the first slice to each other. Then Chayansh fed the second slice to mom and dad. Chanda was heading up to Poorna to give her the third slice. She was standing on the far right of the semicircle.

When she was only a few steps away, something black collided with Poorna and took her with itself.

The black thing and Poorna both were lodged into the cake, destroying it. The first to take a look at the black thing was Chanda. The black thing wasn't a thing, but a person wearing black clothes. It took only a second to realize that it was Shantanu.

Both Poorna and Shantanu were covered in cake and its cream toppings. As he tried to push the cake in order to get up, the cake yielded and toppled over in response. Both of them fell into the cake again, destroying it further. He wiped the cake off his face by his hands. Suddenly he saw something and got up and ran like hell. Following his run, many gazes noticed that he was being chased by a dog. He was running good for someone plastered in cake. The dog had a leash flying around its neck. Someone ran behind both of them and grabbed hold of the leash of the dog and calmed it down.

The party was, in a way, trashed. Most of the people were gathered around him to listen to the back story of his little stunt. Chayansh asked him what happened while he was wiping the cake off. In reply, he started, "Well, I was feeling a little queasy after sometime in the party. So, I went out getting some fresh air. I was walking around some houses when I noticed a dog's bark. I looked behind and saw that dog jump the front wall and charging towards me. So I ran. I ran for some time in the streets and when I couldn't outrun it, I came running here. And the rest is history."

Someone in the crowd said, "You must be around Mr Gupta's house. That dog is his."

Shantanu looked at Chayansh and said, "Sorry, bro, your party got trashed because of me."

"It is okay, Shantu. Parties get trashed sometimes. It's no big deal."

"It's a big deal to me, bro. Listen, I'll leave now. You guys enjoy the party. I'm sorry about the cake, too."

He got up and walked up to Chayansh's mom and dad and apologized to them as well. After that, he walked out of the garden, called an auto and told the driver his destination. The auto sped away.

Inside the auto, he was having a revival of the events that happened. He again saw that he wasn't feeling queasy but he was feeling the urge to urinate. He looked around but couldn't find a restroom so he went outside. After searching for some time he found a dumping area. He went to a corner and started to pee. After finishing, he zipped up his pants and that's when he heard the dog's bark. He saw the dog coming from his left side. So he turned backwards and ran. He was thinking about how it found him. Then it struck him that he must've smelled him from the window on his right.

'Quite an intelligent dog it was.' He thought.

IV

While everyone was listening to Shantanu, Chanda was at the water stand helping Poorna to clean up. She had a box of face wipes she always used to feel refreshing and maintain her skin.

By the time she was half clean, the box was empty, so they were using just water and hands. When she washed off the cake from her hairs, she finally yelled, "*KON THA YE BUNDMAARI DA, KANJAR!?*" Chanda was startled by the sudden increase in her voice.

"Calm down, Poorna, he's my brother's friend."

"So what if he's a friend of your brother? Who does he think he is? You took me away, Chanda, otherwise I would've smacked him so hard he wouldn't feel the dog's bite."

"It was only an accident, Poorna."

"Accident, my foot. There were more than fifty people standing there and he 'accidently' bumped into me only?"

"There is no other possible explanation. He bumped into you by *accident*. You don't know him; he doesn't know you. There is no way he could've done it knowingly."

She knew that she had won the argument by that last statement. She got up from cleaning Poorna's feet and said, "Ok, it's all done. You're clean."

"Is he here yet?"

"Who?"

"Fari, Chanda. Who else would I ask for?"

"Oh, you mean Fareed. No, it seems like he wouldn't be able to make it."

"Ok, thank god."

"You're not mad?"

"I would be mad if I *weren't* in my current situation. I don't want my boyfriend to see me like this. By the way, where is he?"

"I don't know. Possibly he got caught up in studies and forgot to call you."

"No, I meant your brother's friend. Where is he?"

"He must be there in that group. Why are you asking?" Chanda said pointing to the gathered people.

"He at least deserves a heated rebuke for what he did to me." Poorna said and started to walk speedily towards the group. Chanda tried to keep up with her but failed. The pain increased by increasing effort. So she walked at her normal speed hoping to stop her before she causes any menace. While Chanda had travelled $1/4^{th}$ of the distance, she had travelled $9/10^{th}$ of the distance. After a second, she reached the group and started to move people to get to the centre of the group. In the centre, she found only Chayansh wiping off the cake from his pants that fell from Shantanu's body. She asked a direct question, "Where is your friend?"

"Why?" He asked.

"I need to talk to him."

"You're late. He left like five minutes ago."

Poorna clenched her teeth on that reply. She came out of the group the same way she came in. When she came outside, she saw Chanda panting from the effort of walking faster. All her fury vanished in a second. She ran and held Chanda and took her to the nearby chair. She started to wave her hands like a fan. After a few moments, a waiter passed nearby and she grabbed the plate from him, quickly ate all the nuggets and started to fan her with the plate. Chanda, too, enjoyed the pampering for a while.

"Okay, okay, that's enough. I'm okay now." Chanda said.

"What's with you and this boy?" Poorna put the plate down.

"What do you mean?"

"I mean, usually you don't try to interrupt when I try to pick a beef with someone. But this time you were trying to stop me."

"Who said I was trying to stop you?"

"You tried to run to catch up with me, even though you have very little pain tolerance."

Chanda didn't reply. She never thought that she would be caught. Poorna's deduction skills made her remind of Sonia. She smiled. She wished that Sonia was here, too. Poorna would have liked her.

"So, tell me, why were you trying to stop me?" Poorna asked.

This was a question Chanda did not have a prepared answer for. She just remained silent and started to think of a convincible answer. Maybe it was because of her period or maybe she let herself loose, but she noticed something in Chanda's face which she hadn't seen before. It did not take her long to figure out.

"OMG. Oh my god." She said in a low, matter-of-fact tone.

Chanda looked at her. Her eyes were widened and her eyebrows were stretched. Her jaw was in a position to drop. She understood that the truth she had hidden from the whole world was exposed by her simple mistake. There was a relief though that it was her best friend who knew.

"If you say anything to anyone, I will kill you." She said with a look of warning.

In response, Poorna made a gesture of zipping up her lips and throwing the key after locking them. They both smiled.

"Ok, I'll be leaving now. Take care of yourself." She said patting her on the thigh.

She walked a few steps and then turned and asked, "But there is one thing I need to know. What's his name?"

She immediately replied, "*No.* I'm not telling you that. The fact that I have a crush on my brother's friend is enough."

She smiled and gave her a flying kiss. Chanda smiled back. Poorna got out of the marriage garden and called an auto and went back to the hostel.

V

Poorna climbed three flights of stairs and hastily entered room no. 306. She tried to convince herself that she was clean and didn't need a bath. But soon her knack of cleanliness made her throw her clothes off, grab a towel and get ready to wash her clothes before taking a bath. She threw them in the washing machine, poured some water along with detergent and set the timer for 5 minutes. The machine started to wash the clothes by the help of centrifugal force.

With the familiar whirr of washing machine, there was another sound Poorna could hear. It was clear that the sound was in her head. She focused on it and found that it was a song. A song that was being played over and over in her head; She knew that it would continue unless she sang it. She first started humming which eventually turned to singing. This was one of her favourite love songs. She started over because she didn't like to sing songs from the middle. Her voice echoed in the bathroom, making her voice sound more amplified. Her melodious voice, with correct stress on every word, started to reach her ears.

Tu aata hai seene mein,

Jab jab saansen leti hoon.

Tere dil ki galiyon se,

Main har roz guzarti hoon.

Hawa ke jaise chalta hai tu,

Main ret jaise udti hoon.

Kaun tujhe yoon pyaar karega,

Jaise main karti hoon.

While singing the tune, she turned the shower knob and water started to pour down on her. She first let her hair get wet and then she washed her whole body by water. Putting her mouth out of the shower, she continued to sing.

Meri nazar ka safar,

Tujhpe hi aake ruke;

Kehne ko baki hai kya,

Kehna tha jo keh chuke.

Meri nigaahen hai teri nigaahon pe,

Tujhe khabar kya, bekhabar.

Main tujhse hi chup-chup kar,

Teri aankhe padhti hoon.

Kaun tujhe yoon pyaar karega,

Jaise main karti hoon.

She again started to sing the tune. With correct and precise singing, she picked up the soap and started to rub against her bare and cake-smelling body. She quickly washed away the soap and started to shampoo her hair. The tune was ending and another stanza was about to come out of her mouth when she heard these words echo in her bathroom.

"Will you stop singing already?"

She looked around first. With the echo, it was difficult to determine the source of the sound. With her foam-covered hair and naked body, she started to look for possible places where the sound would come from. After searching the whole bathroom, she put her ear on the wall on which the shower was fixed. That was when she clearly heard the voice coming again, this time too loud for her ear.

"I'm the one who spoke. No need to look here and there."

"Who are you?" She said wiggling her finger in her ear.

"It doesn't matter who I am. What matters is your singing."

"What's your problem with my singing?"

"I don't have a problem. It's just that I needed a little silence now."

"Why? Are you writing a novel?"

"No, I'm in the shower and I was thinking about something."

"Well, then think in your room and let me sing, alright."

"No, no, please, I just... need some silence right now. I'm... kind of having a really bad day."

She was about to hurl a finishing argument but stopped at his sentence. The way he said 'really bad day' made her remind of what happened to her in the party; how her boyfriend Fareed didn't even show up. She immediately sympathised with him. As much as she wanted to argue with this voice, she knew that there was a human behind it, suffering as much as she is if not more. Girls are like that;

they sympathise and help others more effectively because they know how to feel.

"Ok. I'm not going to sing. I'll be quiet— But just this once." She said after a sigh.

"Thank you."

She spent the rest of the time standing in the shower. When she was done, the machine had finished its work. She drained the water out from the machine and put the clothes in spin tub to dry them. While the machine was draining the water and drying her clothes, she came out with one towel curled around her head and another was wrapped around her body. She unwrapped and started to wipe herself. She put on her undergarments and fell on the bed. She set an alarm of 7 P.M. in her phone and put her blanket on herself.

As she started to drift off to sleep, there was only one thing going on in her mind. It wasn't the misadventure that happened, or her boyfriend's ignorant behaviour. It was the last comment the stranger's voice passed after a few minutes of silence in the shower.

"I like your voice."

VI

Two minutes before Poorna entered room no. 306, Shantanu was throwing his clothes in the washing machine inside room no. 305. He had put the jacket on the hanger behind his door to send it later to dry clean.

He turned on the shower and stood under it, head first. The water receding from his head felt hotter than the water on his other body parts. The water was soothing cold and made him a little loose. He felt a moment of dizziness but was quick to wake himself back. He put his hand on the wall in front of him and tried to enjoy the water raining on him. He closed his eyes for a second and a picture of the party flashed in his mind, vivid and clear. He opened his eyes again and rubbed them. He felt sleepy.

He again closed his eyes and saw the same picture. There were people distributed around the garden. Chayansh was in the parents' group along with all the friends. People were getting nuggets from the roaming waiters. The buffet was ready but nobody was eating because they were waiting for the cake. Everyone was in that image except Chanda. The realization hit him in a second that it was the time that she was holding his hand. He opened his eyes wide as if he woke up from a nightmare. He felt guilty. He felt guilty to flirt with her and he felt guilty to behave like that. That was when he heard a voice singing. The voice was loud enough to echo in his bathroom.

Tu aata hai seene mein,

Jab jab saansen leti hoon.

Tere dil ki galiyon se,

Main har roz guzarti hoon.

Hawa ke jaise chalta hai tu,

Main ret jaise udti hoon.

Kaun tujhe yoon pyaar karega,

Jaise main karti hoon.

The voice was of a girl's. That was clear. It was melodious and with correct stress on each word but it also made him feel like as if Chanda is singing the song for him. Her face came in front of him as the first stanza ended. The face had the same expression she had when she held his hand. He smelled his hand. He somehow could recognize that his hand smelled different. After the end of the tune, another stanza echoed in his bathroom.

Meri nazar ka safar,

Tujhpe hi aake ruke;

Kehne ko baki hai kya,

Kehna tha jo keh chuke.

Meri nigaahen hai teri nigaahon pe,

Tujhe khabar kya, bekhabar.

Main tujhse hi chup-chup kar,

Teri aankhe padhti hoon.

Kaun tujhe yoon pyaar karega,

Jaise main karti hoon.

The voice again started to hum the tune. He felt guiltier with each sentence. Chanda's face while talking to him, then holding his hand and when he freed his hand; all the faces came and faded like a fast slideshow. He couldn't take it anymore. He yelled out, "Will you quit singing already?"

The voice was loud, even for him. The tune had stopped. He knew that it hasn't stopped because he told her to but because she wasn't expecting a voice. After a few seconds, he said, "I'm the one who spoke. No need to look here and there."

"Who are you?"

"It doesn't matter who I am. What matters is your singing."

"What's your problem with my singing?"

"I don't have a problem. It's just that I needed a little silence now."

"Why? Are you writing a novel?"

"No, I'm in the shower and I was thinking about something."

"Well, then think in your room and let me sing, alright."

"No, no, please, I just... need some silence right now. I'm... kind of having a really bad day."

There was no reply for a few moments. Even though he knew that his statement was lame, he couldn't have said anything better. He was pondering whether he said it with enough emotion or not when the voice echoed in his bathroom, "Ok, I'm not going to sing. I'll be quiet—but just this once."

He replied, "Thank you." and stood in the shower for a few minutes. He wanted to use soap but he was feeling so sleepy that he thought that he will just wash himself with water. He turned the knob and the shower stopped. He grabbed his towel hanging on the back of the bathroom door.

Wiping himself, he noticed how the atmosphere was silent. He put his ear to the wall. He could listen regular unending muffling voices which he knew were of the shower running. He found himself feeling indebted to her. He thought that he should say something. So he said the sentence he regretted from the moment he said it, because he felt it was cheesy and kind of lame.

"I like your voice."

VII

Three days after this fiasco, Poorna entered room no. 306 of A & A girls' hostel. She was dressed in a white, cut-sleeves t-shirt with a denim jacket over it, wearing red coloured jeggings with low heel sandals. She had applied make up which had started to mix with the sweat on her face. The mascara in her eyes was just as it was, but the hair had become from a bun to a messy hairdo with the speed walking she did. The purse dangled from her arm as she tried to put the key into the lock. The lock wasn't complying with her hands which seemed like they were shaking. She finally managed to unlock the gate and closed it with full force. She walked into the room but something pulled her back. She looked back to see that her purse was only halfway in. She opened the door and threw the purse on the bed and closed the door with a loud bang. She walked a few steps and threw herself on the bed.

Her face was flushed red with anger. She undid her bun and spread her hair on the bed. She knew that she would be brought to tears if she didn't do something to distract herself. With clenched teeth, she took off her denim jacket along with the t-shirt and threw them on the bed. She took off her jeggings as fast as she could without tearing them and headed off to the bathroom. She thought a long shower will calm her down or even if it didn't, at least her tears will not be visible to her.

She turned the knob and the cold water started to rain down on her. She felt an inexplicable calm and also something weird on her chest and between her thighs. She opened her eyes to see that she had not taken off her undergarments. She hastily took them off and then started to enjoy the water with her eyes closed. She stood there in the shower in the same position for a few minutes until her torpor was disturbed by a voice.

Teri yaari, badi pyaari,

Par main bhi, hoon khiladi,

No, aata nahi,

Aata nahi,

Aata nahi,

Mujhko chupana. O. O.

Din bhar tu, pyaar chahe,

Raat ko baby, ruth jaaye,

No, aata nahi,

Aata nahi,

Aata nahi,

Mujhko manana.

So let's break up,

O meri jaan.

Let's break up,

O maan jaa.

Teri-meri kabhi nahin banni,

O jaane de na.

The words stung in her ears. It made her all the more dislike the voice. It was like her boyfriend Fari was singing all this. That thought alone made her feel guilty. So what if he didn't show up for a date? So what if he didn't have the guts to tell her directly? That doesn't lessen his love for her. How can she doubt the one she loves?

She felt some warm water along with the cold water on her face. The warm water was coming out of her eyes. She thanked herself for her idea of crying in a shower. She had done this before and it had been effective. Meanwhile, the song continued again.

Dikh jaaye, jo haseena,

Choot jaata, hai paseena,

Basically,

Basically,

Basically hoon main kamina.

Woah-oh

Tu bhi kahan, kam hai baby,

Kabhi seedhi, kabhi tedhi,

Basically,

Basically,

Basically tu bhi kamini.

So let's...

"SHUT UP!"

Poorna shouted at the top of her lungs. Of course, the singing stopped. She was taking heavy breaths while feeling more of the warm water on her cheeks which came out of her eyes. The shower and the silence went on for a few minutes and then came a male voice, "Are you okay?"

She could tell by the voice that the boy on the other side was genuinely frightened and worried at the same time. She cleared her throat and tried to speak in a voice that was not hoarse or breathy, "I'm fine."

"Your actions tell a whole different story."

"Well, I didn't want you to sing. That song gets on my nerves."

"Okay, no problem, I'll sing a different song."

"Is it really necessary for you to sing?"

"Yes, it is. And it is your fault."

"It's my fault? How is it my fault?"

"After hearing you sing in the shower, I also found my habit of singing in the shower returning to me."

Silence.

"Is it convincing enough or should I talk more?"

"Fine, sing away."

"Thank you."

There was silence in the shower. But after a few seconds, the boy on the other side began to sing.

I do as you say,

Want it the other way?

Coffees on Saturdays,

Breakups on Sundays.

It's like...

I do as you say,

Want it the other way?

Coffees on Saturdays,

Breakups on Sundays.

Phir meri jaan,

Badhega faasla,

Ho kar judaa,

Phir milega koi naya.

"Okay, stop." She said

"What's happened now?" The voice sounded irritated.

"Nothing, just... let's not sing at all."

"Why not; you just gave me permission to sing."

"Well, I take it back. Ok?"

"No, you can't. I need to sing."

"Why?"

"Because if I don't sing; then these songs are going to be stuck in my head for the whole day. I wouldn't be able to concentrate on anything."

"Ok, so take a holiday today."

"No, I can't bunk classes."

"A day doesn't make a difference."

"I still am singing, whether you like it or not."

"No, no, no. I just need some silence right now, please."

"Why do you need silence for? Are you meditating?"

"No, I just need some silence for the same reason you had that day."

"Oh, so you had a bad day today, huh?"

"Yes." She said in an annoyed tone.

"All right, I'll stay silent for today; but only this once and only because you did the same for me."

"Ok, thank you."

"Don't mention it."

VIII

A week after, Shantanu was about to take off his clothes when he heard the singing from the other side. She was singing the first Spanish lines of the song 'senorita'. He smiled at her efforts on trying to sing them right. It was the sixth time him and her were showering at the same time. It had become more of a habit for him to hear her voice nearly every day. He knew he had to interrupt her before she goes into her singer mode. He shouted, "Silence!"

"What?" her reply came immediately.

"You can't sing today."

"Why can't I?"

"Because I want to sing and you have been singing for three days in a row."

"Can you sing tomorrow? I really want to sing today."

"No. I want to sing today and I can. It's only fair."

"Fine, Have it your way."

"Thank you."

He walked to the shower and turned the knob. He started to shower his legs first and started to hum a tune of Ghulam Ali's ghazal. When he washed his body up to his stomach, he sprouted the words out.

Chupke, chupke, raat din,

Aansoo bahana, yaad hai,

Humko, ab tak aashiqui ka woh,

Zamaana, yaad hai- hai.

Chupke, chupke, raat din,

Aansoo bahana, yaad hai,

Humko, ab tak aashiqui ka woh,

Zamaana, yaad hai- hai.

On the other side, Poorna didn't like the slow tone of the song. It was a joy-killer for her 'happy go lucky' mood. But she knew that she had to bear it for the day since she was singing for three days straight. She applied soap to her body as the song continued.

Tujhse milte hi,

Who kuch bebaak ho jaana mera,

Tujhse milte hi,

Who kuch bebaak ho jaana mera,

Aur,

Tera, daanto mein woh,

Ungli dabana yaad hai.

Humko ab tak aashiqui ka woh,

Zamana yaad hai.

The song continued in the monotonous, slow fashion. Poorna didn't remember much of it. But when the song ended, she shouted to Shantanu, "From now on, we are going to alternate the singing."

"...But why? This is good."

"Yes, but I want a fair chance to irritate you."

"What?"

"Yes, your song was irritating. Couldn't you choose a much slower song?"

"It's Ghulam Ali. He's slow *and* fantastic."

"Well, I prefer fast."

"Then you'll have to wait for your turn."

"That is exactly what I'm saying. Let's alternate the singing. One day I'll sing my tunes and the next day you'll sing yours."

"Hm. It doesn't sound like a bad idea. I can do that." The reply came after a little silence.

"Alright, so tomorrow I'm singing."

"Ok, great. Just don't be vengeful."

"Fine, I'll have mercy on you." She said with a little laugh.

IX

Ever since they started that arrangement, both Shantanu and Poorna became everyday bathers. At first, they only sung when they were showering at the same time, but soon they co-ordinated their timings. Now they both had started to go to the bathroom at the same time. They had even started to talk about their personal lives. Both of them didn't get close yet, but they knew and felt a bond forming between them.

The day was a Sunday. On Sundays, they both had decided that they will shower together later in the noon, since they both are late sleepers. Shantanu was lying in his bed wide awake. He had woken up earlier but didn't feel like getting up. He looked at the clock and saw it was 11:30 a.m. He had been awake for nearly two hours and was half an hour away from the prescheduled shower singing. It had been three days since he had been waking up in the middle of his siestas. He knew that something was troubling him, but he couldn't exactly pinpoint the reason. He sat up on his bed and started to think what could be troubling him.

First, the image of his monthly exam's result came in where he had around 42%. He had viewed his result around four days ago. That time, standing in the hall near the notice board, wearing the white shirt and blackish-grey pants with the ID card dangling from his neck— the Allen's uniform— he felt his whole world shift. After all, it's not easy to see something change that fast— even if it's your grades.

Second, he saw himself in Chayansh's home. After the result, Chayansh was excited to tell his result to his mother. He had achieved 95% and was in the top 100. Chanda, too, had excelled in the test and achieved 96%. She, too, was in top 100. He had called him at his home to celebrate. Shantanu had merely put a jacket on top of his regular clothes and was waiting for both of them.

After a few minutes, both of them showed up. Chayansh was wearing a blue T-shirt which had a picture of Chris Hemsworth. Along with that, He was wearing a black pant from which a 2000 rupee note was peeping in the left pocket.

On the other hand, Chanda had dressed more properly. She was wearing a turquoise shirt and light blue jeans along with wood-brown heels. They all acknowledged how good-looking they were and went out to the city mall. In the auto-rickshaw, Shantanu noticed that her dress was a little tighter that she used to wear regularly. 'Maybe she saw them fitting for celebration.' He thought.

Thirdly, at the mall, they all enjoyed to their heart's content. For the moment, even Shantanu forgot his grief and enjoyed with them. The film they saw wasn't much, but the popcorn was good. While they were at the domino's waiting for a large size pizza, Chanda asked him to show her the restroom. He obliged and took her to the first floor where they turned left near the stairs. There were the restrooms for both men and women. She rushed in for the women's restroom while he waited outside, just for courtesy. While waiting, he heard Chanda calling for him. He looked back to see her peeking out of the door of the women's restroom. He looked around before walking up to her.

"What happened?" he asked.

"Um, there has been a problem."

"Yes, I sense that. What is the problem?"

"Well, don't laugh," She hesitantly spoke, "I, uh, I seemed to have torn my jeans."

"What?" he chuckled, "How did you tear one of the *toughest* fabrics of clothing?"

"It was a little tight, okay?"

"Okay, so what do you want me to do?"

"Get some pins. I might be able to pull it back and hold it till we get home."

"Okay."

Shantanu walked straight to the big bazaar and asked where he could find safety pins. He bought a total of 30 pins since he didn't know how many would be needed.

But there was one problem. The big bazaar does not allow the customers to exit the same way they came in. So, he had to circle back to the main entrance and walk up to the first floor. He saw the door was closed, so he knocked. Chanda opened the door a peek and he handed her all the pins.

"How many pins have you brought?"

"I think there are 30."

"I didn't need that many pins!"

"Use as many as you need and give the rest back to me. I'll use them as toothpicks." He joked.

She made a face and took the pins and closed the door. He waited outside for some more time.

"Um, Shantu?" She called again.

He turned to find that she was still peeking from behind the door. He walked closer and asked, "What?"

"I'm not sure if I did it correctly, and the height of the mirrors and the tight jeans isn't really helping. So, can you... check for me?"

"Check what for you?"

"If it's done well." She said and opened the door. She looked perfectly fine. There was nothing wrong with her jeans. There weren't even any pins. It was when she turned around that he saw what was wrong. The jeans were torn from the middle of the butt portion, just below the waistline. And there were several pins arbitrarily pushed through all through the long tear. They held the torn ends efficiently but they were very unsuccessful in pulling them together.

"Is it okay?"She asked.

"It looks like some sort of bizarre, cringe fashion."

"I didn't ask how it looked. Is it covering the tear?"

"No, it isn't. Why didn't you take the jeans off first and then did this?"

"Do you know how hard it is to fit in these jeans?"

"Okay, point taken." As soon as he finished saying, an idea struck in his mind. He took off his jacket, held both arms of the jacket and held her from the waist. Chanda stopped abruptly by his actions, feeling electricity at his touch. He pulled her closer and tied the arms of the jacket slowly around her waist, all the while holding her. He tried his best not to make it sexual but there was no way it couldn't be that. After he was done, he let go of her.

"Shantu, we're in public." Chanda whispered.

She only turned slowly and looked at him. It was strange. She neither looked furious or shocked. She was smiling rather mischievously. It was like she had expected this but not like the way it happened. But soon Shantanu came back to his senses and replied, also whispering, "Well, now, nobody will see that tear."

Soon they both realized that they were attracting a lot of attention. So they parted and walked back to the domino's. He didn't remember rest of the day but when the auto-rickshaw reached their house— and Chayansh had hurried off because he needed to use the washroom— Chanda turned to him and started to unwind the knot of jacket arms. Shantanu stopped her and said, "Don't worry, you can return this to me later."

"Thank you." she said with a smile and tied the knots back. She leaned towards him and kissed him on the cheek. Then she whispered in his ear, "You are a sweet and respectful one, Shantu. I'm glad to have you."

Without thinking, he replied, "So am I." After that, he directed the auto to his room and slept for around two hours. It was only after he woke up did he realize what happened in detail. That night, he didn't sleep.

Suddenly, his alarm clock brought him back to the present. He looked at his phone. It was 11:55 a.m. He turned off the alarm and sat up in bed, still tired. He was deciding whether he should shower today or just fall back asleep.

X

After reasoning with himself for a while, Shantanu got up, took off his clothes and grabbed his towel and went inside the bathroom. He felt the distance between his bed and bathroom much greater than before. Whatever he was doing felt like a very hard work. When the mind is tired, body ceases to work. He hung the towel on the back of the door and stepped inside. He turned the knob and stepped back from the stream of shower. Firstly, he washed his legs and gradually, brought his whole body under.

He just stood under the shower with his head bowed down. The water was running down from the back of his neck, through the spine and down to his legs— leaving his face untouched by the water. He was rethinking that entire day.

He knew he couldn't have done much about the marks. But couldn't he have covered Chanda in a way that doesn't send a wrong signal? Why did he think he was allowed to do whatever he did? Why did she look at him like that and say that she was glad to have him?

These were one of the many questions Shantanu was struggling to find answers of. He felt guilty. He couldn't tell exactly of what, but he felt guilty. He was in the middle of the process of self-reasoning when a voice came from the other end, "So, we got an early bird."

"Yeah, I thought I should finish this as quickly as possible." He said trying his best to sound normal.

"Well, you're not that lucky. I still came and I'm still singing."

"Good. Finish it quickly."

Firstly, he heard the sound of shower and then he heard her clear her throat. After a few seconds, her voice started to echo in his bathroom.

Got this feeling for you,

Inside;

And then back on the tears,

I cried.

Tu hai bhatakta jugnoo koi,

Mai toh andhere ki hoon pari,

Tu hai awaara toofan koi,

Mai udta hua tinka sahi.

Aaj apna Milan ho gaya,

Kis khwaab ne, chup-chap se,

Mera badan choo liya.

Kis khwaab ne, chup-chap se,

Mera badan choo liya.

Tu hai bhatakta jugnoo koi,

Mai toh andhere ki hoon pari.

Got this feeling for you,

Inside,

And then back on the tears,

I cried.

The song brought a clear image of what happened between him and Chanda. He remembered everything in detail. Her face, her response and the aftermath played on and on like a video loop. Poorna's subtle and correct singing didn't help at all. It was like Chanda's feelings for him had just been constructed into a song. Meanwhile, the song continued.

Baahon mein leke,

Mujhko sikha de,

Sang main tere naach loon,

Sab dar mere,

Aaj bhula de,

Indradhanush choo loon,

jaise koi,

mor hai naache,

pehli bahaaron mein,

main ek panchi,

sehma-sehma,

pehli udaan bhare,

tune mujhe udnaa sikhladiya,

kaisa haseen ye jaadu kiya,

kis khwaab ne, chup-chap se,

mera badan choo liya,

kis khwaab ne, chup-chap se,

mera badan choo liya.

The words stung like acid in his ears. The shower drops felt like thousands of needles on his body. Shantanu put his hand on the wall in front of him and bowed his head. His head felt heavy. He closed his eyes and everything that happened, seemed to roll by right in front of his eyes. It felt fast, but still it was slow enough for him to see and notice every detail.

That's when it happened. He felt drops of warm water cascading down his face. This time, he let it flow. He didn't hold back. The song made him weak. So weak that he couldn't stand. He sat down under the shower and folded his legs and buried his face between his knees and cried.

He cried because he didn't know what to do. He cried because he felt that he was doing wrong by giving her false hope. He cried because he knew that he was playing with an innocent heart. He can't feed her heart false emotions but he couldn't break her heart as well. She would get over it, but then she'll lose herself along with what Shantanu liked in her.

The song continued and finished after a while. Poorna got out of the shower while humming the tune of another song. Meanwhile, he sat in the shower crying, asking a question that he couldn't find an answer to.

God, isn't there any other way?

XI

Six days later, Shantanu was preparing to go for a bath. He picked up his towel and looked at the clock. It was almost 8:00 a.m. He picked up his phone too and headed for the shower. He opened his door and stepped inside. He put his phone on the soap-holder and put the soap down on the floor. Then he went to the door and closed it.

With closing the door, another sound came. It was the sound of opening the door on Poorna's side. He smiled. He went under the shower and waited for her to start the talk. But instead, she started to hum the tune of a song from the movie 'Dear Zindagi'. Maybe she didn't notice I'm here, he thought. He cleared his throat and made a voice loud enough for her to hear. The humming stopped. Then her voice echoed in his ears, "I didn't notice you're here."

"I figured that. So tell me, what's your mood like today?"

"Well, I don't think I have to tell you that. My humming must've told you already."

"You were humming?" He tried to sound surprised.

"Yes."

"So, what song were you humming?"

"...'Tu hi hai' from Dear Zindagi."

"Ooh, sounds like you're in a lovey-dovey mood."

"So it would seem."

"Alright, so that's what we're going to have on the playlist today."

"What're you going to sing?"

"You'll know soon enough. I've brought karaoke with me."

"...Karaoke?"

"Yes." He said and started to find the karaoke version of the song he had downloaded on his phone. After a few seconds, the song started playing. Shantanu first sang the interlude and then he started singing.

Bheegi-bheegi sadakon pe main,

Tera intezaar karoon;

Dheere-dheere dil ki zameen ko,

Tere hi naam karoon.

Khud ko main yoon kho doon,

Ke phir na kabhi paaon,

Haule-haule Zindagi ko,

Ab tere hawale karoon.

Sanam re, Sanam re,

Tu mera Sanam hua re,

Sanam re, Sanam re,

Tu mera Sanam hua re,

Karam re, karam re,

Tera mujhpe karam hua re.

Sanam re, Sanam re,

Tu mera Sanam hua re.

That was when the rhythm of the song changed from classical to rock. The sound of rock guitar came on. Shantanu turned the knob right at the part where the song's overall tune changed. Water started to fall on him in little drops as He held his hands up like he was holding a guitar and playing it in a rock concert. With that, he sang the interlude. With that going on for a few seconds, the words again came out of his mouth.

Tere kareeb jo hone laga hoon,

Toh toote saare bharam re;

Sanam re, Sanam re,

Tu mera Sanam hua re,

Sanam re, Sanam re,

Tu mera Sanam hua re.

Then, again he sang the interlude. On the other side, Poorna was really enjoying the song. She loved Arijit's songs and He was singing it with such flair that it just fuelled her happy mood. She was actually dancing when the tune changed. The day felt perfect. A date was scheduled by her otherwise ignorant boyfriend Fareed. She had woken up early and energetic without the help of an alarm clock. And she had gotten the news that another member was going to enter their joint family. Her cousin *bhabhi* was pregnant. And now, Shantanu was singing her one of her favourites. While she kept dancing, the song continued.

Baadalon ki tarah hi toh,

Tune mujhpe saaya kiya hai,

Baarishon ki tarah hi toh,

Tune khushiyon se bhigaya hai,

Aandhiyon ki tarah hi toh,

Tune hosh ko udaya hai;

Mera muqaddar sawara hai yoon,

Naya sawera jo laya hai tu,

Tere sang hi bitaane hai muhjko,

Mere saare janam re.

Poorna couldn't hold her voice inside herself now. There was too much happiness for her to handle. She had been dancing to the song all along but now she wanted to sing while dancing. When he sang the line she also chimed in with correct gaps and stresses.

Sanam re, sanam re,

Sanam re, sanam re,

Tu mera Sanam hua re,

Sanam re, sanam re,

Sanam re, sanam re,

Tu mera Sanam hua re,

Karam re, karam re,

Karam re, karam re,

Tera mujhpe karam hua re,

Sanam re, sanam re,

Tu mera Sanam hua re.

Then, he started singing the interlude while playing the imaginary rock guitar in his hands. He sang the interlude with dexterity and whenever he had to take a breath, he used the gaps in between. Around 18 seconds into the interlude, Poorna started singing while Shantanu kept singing the interlude with his best.

Mere sanam re, mera hua re,

Tera karam re, muhjpe hua yeh.

Mere sanam re, mera hua re,

Tera karam re, mujhpe hua yeh.

With those words, there was the sound of a single guitar cord and then everything went silent. On one side, Poorna was feeling extremely relieved and happy with what she did. On the other side, Shantanu was feeling shivers down his spine with distant ringing in his ears. It was a feeling he had termed as 'musical high'. He had sung this song many times but he never achieved this feeling. He used to get this 'musical high' when he listened to the songs, but never while singing them. When the song ended, both of them felt worked up but not exhausted.

For the next few minutes, the only sound in the bathrooms was of the shower. Unable to bear the silence anymore, he spoke, "You were the one that was singing in between, right?"

She knew it was more of a statement than a question, but she answered it like one. "Yes, it was me."

"You sing Arijit very well." She said after a few seconds of silence.

"Well, he's my favourite."

"He's my favourite, too."

"Which one of his songs you like the most?"

"'Sanam re' is my favourite."

"So... how did I do? Was I okay or did I mess it up?"

"No, no. You were okay. You were very good actually. I literally got shivers down my spine."

"What? I got shivers, too."

"Does it feel unusual to you? I mean, I've only got such spine shivers when I'm listening to songs, not while singing them."

"Well, to be honest, it *does* feel unusual to me as well. But I think that it's not bad to get musical highs while singing."

"...Musical high?"

"I'm talking about the spine shivers that we both got. I call them 'musical highs'"

"Oh." She said with a little laugh.

Some more minutes went by in silence. Shantanu was done with his showering. While wiping his body with a towel, he said, "Are you still there?"

"Yes, I'm here."

"I just want to say that you sing very well."

"I know that. Why tell me?"

"It's nothing. It's just... I have a proposal."

"Don't tell me you're on your knees."

"No... Not *that* proposal."

Poorna laughed out loud in response.

"Listen, listen. What I'm proposing is that instead of alternating our singing, why don't we start singing together?"

"I don't follow."

"Look, before we used to sing alternatively, now what I'm saying is that we should sing duet songs regularly. We already shower together, so let's sing together as well."

"Not a bad idea, I'll think about it." She said teasing him.

"Oh, come on. Please?"

"Alright, that's fine. But the selection of song will remain alternative."

"I don't follow." Shantanu said mockingly.

"Don't use my lines against me."

"Ok, I got it. I chose the song today, so you'll choose tomorrow."

"Alright, I will."

"Choose wisely."

"Live well."

"What? What does that mean?"

He only got Poorna's laugh and the sound of closing of door as a response.

XII

Poorna's date was set in Mahavir Nagar- 1st itself. Approximately two streets on the way to the City mall, or around 2 kilometres, a place named 'Village 69' exists. It was a terrace restaurant which was set on the terrace of a house. From outside, Village 69 looked like an over-glorified hut set high on a pole; but from inside Village 69 lived up to its reputations. The village house theme worked its modern restaurant theme to its perfection. Village 69 looked like some sort of tropical getaway.

After paying the auto-rickshaw, she walked up to the spiral metal staircase on which Poorna usually feared of falling. Carefully taking her steps, she reached at the top and was welcomed by the owner sitting at the counter on her right side. She turned left and sat on one of the fancy plastic chairs which were either red or orange in colour. She was sitting at a table for four. She put down her purse on the table and picked up the menu.

After looking at the menu for a few seconds, she decided what she will order. She was going to order two macaroni pastas with red sauce, Fareed's favourite. She put the menu down and started to wait for Fareed.

Fareed was her batch mate before he became her boyfriend. His full name was Fareed Iqbal Jafri. She had met him during the orientation programme. Their meeting was brief, but both of them knew substantial information about each other after that— like she knew that his mother was dead before he even crossed 5 years of age. He belonged to Gorakhpur, U.P. His hobbies were dancing, sketching and photography, etc. Also, she had told him much about her— like she had told him that she was from a small village in Ludhiana, Punjab. She wasn't much close to her mother than her father who died when she was 13. Her hobbies were singing (not competitively), dancing and reading fiction, etc.

After that, they both got enrolled in the same batch, thanks to the co-ed classes of IIT. She knew that every boy hated waking up early in the morning. But when Fareed changed his batch from evening batch to morning batch because of her, she knew that both of them would go a long way. Fareed did all the things to be near her. He used to sit on her right in the class, holding her hand under the seat occasionally. He worked hard to mix up her gang with his gang so that they could go out together more easily. He also asked her out to lunches and dinner, even though she couldn't identify all of them as 'dates' for some unknown reason. After a few outings, they were girlfriend-boyfriend. But as time passed, she had started to notice a real change in Fareed. His sudden inclination towards his studies and career had seemed to block her out of his life. But this date had proved that she wasn't blocked out of his life.

She looked at her clock. It was almost 8:00 p.m. She pulled out her phone from the purse and texted Fareed asking where was he, to which he replied that he was stuck in traffic and will come soon. She understood. After all, she lived in Mahavir nagar- 1st and Fareed lived in Talwandi. It is a long way and the roads are always populous.

"Hi." A voice came from Poorna's right. She turned and saw that it was Chanda. She slid the chair and got up and hugged Chanda. While she was hugging her, she noticed that Shantanu was standing behind her, or more accurately near the counter. Poorna recognized him almost instantly as the boy who bumped into her at Chanda and Chayansh's birthday party, dumping her into the cake. She was about to say something sarcastic but then she remembered that he was also Chanda's crush, so she thought that it was best not to say anything. She decided to pretend that she didn't know him.

"What are you doing here?" Poorna asked breaking the hug.

"I could just about ask you the same question."

"Well, I'm on a date." She replied shyly.

"Ooh! That's great. How about making it a double date?"

"Setting up a Double date? I don't think that Fari will like it."

"Oh, he'll love it. Besides," she leaned in and whispered, "My one is too shy. Help me out, Poorna." As she moved away, she said aloud, "So, should we do it?"

"Let's do it." Poorna said reluctantly.

Both Shantanu and Chanda sat on adjacent chairs and Poorna sat in front of them with the chair beside her empty. After getting comfortable, Chanda asked, "So what have you ordered?"

"Oh, I haven't ordered anything yet. I thought that I would order once Fari gets here." Poorna replied looking at the entrance.

"That's okay. Would you mind if we order now? I'm famished."

"No, no, that's completely okay. You both go ahead and order."

"Okay." she said and turned to him. "So, what'll we be having tonight?"

"...whatever you order." he replied. He said it in such a small voice that it was almost inaudible to Poorna. She was astonished that a *boy* could be that shy.

"How do you fancy Manchurian; with gravy or without?" Chanda's tone was still enthusiastic.

He momentarily looked at her, and then first looking down and then at the menu, he said in that small, flat tone, "Either one is good."

Poorna raised her eyes and smiled lopsidedly. She looked at Shantanu. He was wearing a plain crimson coloured shirt with its arms folded up till the elbow with a grey jeans and black sports shoes. Then, she looked at Chanda. She was wearing a sky blue top with big white polka dots on it along with light blue jeans and pink bellies. Then she looked at herself. She was wearing a black tank top with a see-through off shoulder crop top over it along with tight black jeans and black heels of moderate height. She was now starting to think that she should've dressed a little more lightly.

Chanda called the waiter and ordered two Manchurians with gravy and two Pinãcoladas. As the waiter was about to leave, Poorna stopped him and ordered two macaroni pastas with red sauce. She thought it would be better that when Fari would reach, he wouldn't have to wait for food.

It didn't take too long for the food to reach. The waiter brought all the items on a big plate and started putting them one by one. First he put the Manchurians and then the Pinăcoladas and then he put one plate of pasta and started to leave. Seeing just one plate, she stopped the waiter and told him that she had ordered two plates. The waiter looked in his diary and apologized for the mistake and went back to get her another plate. She had decided to wait for Fari but with the insistence of Chanda, she agreed to eat.

The conversation seemed to only exist between her and Chanda. Shantanu was quietly eating and giving facial reactions to whatever they were talking about. This irritated Poorna— even though she couldn't explain why. Five minutes into the conversation, Chanda's phone started to ring. She excused herself and went out to take the call.

Meanwhile, Poorna's curiosity had reached its peak. She was eager to know almost everything about this boy in front of her and what made Chanda fall for him. As soon as she went out the gate, possibly sitting on the stairs to talk, she leaned in and said, "You do know that you're on a date, right?"

"Yes." He said confoundedly.

"Then why are you acting like you're some kind of slave she bought? Don't you know..." she was about to say *'she loves you'* but stopped and said, "... how to behave on a date?"

"Uh, unfortunately, I've never been to a date." The voice was still too little to be deciphered correctly, but she had somehow listened.

"Well, then, I too feel sorry for you, I really do. But at least try to be a little talkative and social for her— or even just fake being social, that will work too."

"Why are you so hell-bent on making me acting social?"

"Because I see that she does not like that you're not talking beyond monosyllabic replies."

"But she seems so enthusiastic."

"She's a very great actor. I mean, I only know for a few days that you've been her crush since 8th class."

"What?" he asked. Poorna instantly regretted what she said. She bit her tongue. He frowned.

"What did you just say?" He pressed with a sudden change in his tone of voice.

Before he could press the matter further, Chanda stepped back into the restaurant and joined them at the table. The dinner went as usual but Poorna noticed that she *did* help her friend. She was sure that at least he will now look at her from a different perspective.

XIII

After the dinner, Shantanu and Chanda stepped out of Village 69. As soon as he had heard that Chanda had a crush on him since 8th class, he couldn't believe his own ears. All this while he had a doubt about her liking him, but now that that girl had laid it all out, he was sure. While climbing down the stairs, he almost slipped twice. When they both reached the bottom of the stairs, she asked him, "Are you okay?"

How do I answer that? How can I be okay? No crush lasts that long. She freaking loves me. He thought and replied, "Yeah, I'm okay. I was just lost in thought."

"What were you thinking about?" Chanda asked jokingly.

"...You." He replied absent-mindedly.

As soon as he realized what he had just said, he turned to take it back. But with one look at Chanda, he knew that it was impossible to undo what he had done. Even though there wasn't much light, he could tell that her cheeks had flushed red. They both stood there for a few seconds, looking at each other from the corners of their eyes. She said to him, "Let's take a walk back to your hostel." He couldn't do anything except complying.

Instead of going the usual way, Chanda started to walk inside the street labyrinth. Shantanu followed her. When they both were side-by-side, she reached out and held his hand. She felt electricity and Goosebumps started to form up on her skin. She slid herself closer to him and when their arms brushed, He felt her Goosebumps.

He looked at her hand first and then at Chanda. She smiled in response. Her smile was one of those 'first' smiles; like a smile that appears when someone tries something for the first time. A little shy, a little scared, yet grateful for trying. But her eyes told a different story. Her eyes were filled with a sense of surety and euphoria. It almost felt as if she was sending out some kind of vibes and now were expecting the same ones in return. As soon as Shantanu looked in her eyes, he had started to feel the vibes. If it would've been any other night, he wouldn't have understood, but tonight, he knew that she loved him.

It took him a few seconds to realize that both of them have been standing under a streetlight for at least a minute. He pulled his eyes away and started to walk. After approximately 38 seconds of walking, Chanda suddenly stopped and tightened her grip which made him stop. He turned to look at her. He found that she was already looking at him dreamy-eyed.

"I have a question to ask you."

"What is it?" He sounded like he was lost somewhere.

"Do you know when a crush turns into love?"

'I know why you are asking me this.' He thought. "Scientifically, a crush lasts 4 months maximum. So, a crush must turn into love after 4 months."

She laughed a little at his response.

"Scientifically, correct but generally, wrong."

"What do you mean?" His interest was awoken.

"Well, science has a bad habit of analysing everything on its own terms and conditions. If love is an emotion, how could science bound it in numbers?"

"So what should be the answer to this question *emotionally*?"

Chanda's amused look was replaced by another look. It was a look that Shantanu had never seen on her face. Her smile had disappeared but she didn't look sad or angry. Her grip on his hand had tightened. He felt her getting closer. But there was something about what was happening. He felt like stopping her but for some reason he didn't. There are parts of us that always want what either can't be or shouldn't be ours. They are not our alter egos or split personalities, but actually are parts of ours that lay deep in our consciousness like dormant seeds.

Chanda was so close to him that he could feel her breath. Her breath smelled of peppermint. A mouth spray, of course. But tonight, there was something different about it. It made him feel special. He had heard the term 'impossible relations' but now, standing here, he wanted it more than anything the world could've offered him that time.

"Do you know when a crush turns into love?" Chanda whispered; her lips only centimetres away from Shantanu's.

He only shook his head slowly.

"It's when she feels Goosebumps *every* time *he* touches her." She whispered and leaned in. Seeing her getting close, He closed his eyes. He didn't care what his conscience would say. He didn't care about Chayansh's reaction to this. He didn't care how impossible this relationship was. All he cared about was him and her, in this moment, reaching out to each other's deepest desires.

That was when it happened. Big drops of rain started to pour down on them. Both were suddenly pulled out of the trance they were enjoying. Shantanu felt the emptiness that comes after waking up from an ecstatic dream. He looked up with a look of disgust on his face, as if cursing the rain. The rain was sudden and fierce. The drops were hitting them like small pieces of glass. When he looked back at Chanda, she was still looking up— only, she looked actually happy. She opened her arms and smiled fully, all the while looking up. She looked like some heroine about to dance in the rain. He looked at her and smiled a guilt smile. He would've looked at her for a long time if the rain drops weren't constantly reminding him.

"We should find a roof or something to stand under, otherwise we'll catch cold." He said.

Chanda looked at him as if he had said something alien to her. After a few seconds, she agreed and they started to run to find shelter. Soon they both were standing under a shade. Both of them were soaking wet. She was looking at Shantanu from the corners of her eyes. He was busy reconciling the events that happened and would've happened. He had reached afar in his mind when he felt a gaze. He turned to see it was Chanda looking at him with the same dreamy eyes. It was then that he realized that it was not only him who was visualizing ahead. He smiled. She smiled back. They both would've looked at each other for too long if she hadn't sneezed.

"My hostel is near. You can dry yourself there." Shantanu offered.

"No, I'll just call Chayansh to pick me up."

"Tell him to bring the car to my hostel. He'll arrive while you dry yourself."

Chanda smiled at his courteous nature. Any other person would get awkward, but not Shantanu. That was what she always admired in him. She nodded in yes. He walked out from under the shade and she followed.

XIV

It took them roughly 12 minutes to reach A & A boys' hostel. At the entry gate, the guard initially didn't allow her to enter, but Shantanu's approach with the guard and a little bribe worked and Chanda was allowed on the condition that Ms. Warden should not know about it.

Once inside the room 305, he ran and opened his cupboard and fished two towels out of it. He gestured to the bathroom and said, "Here, you should dry yourself first. Put your clothes in the washing machine and then in the dryer and shower while I bring some dry clothes for you."

"Okay." She said and started to walk to the bathroom. Once she closed the door, Shantanu started to unbutton his shirt. Then he produced another towel and took off all his clothes and left a pile of them outside on the left of the bathroom door. He wrapped the towel around his waist and started to look for clothes. He was wondering if his clothes would fit Chanda. He walked to the bathroom door and knocked twice.

"Yes?" She replied.

"What's your size?"

"What?" She said chuckling.

"I mean what size clothes do you wear?"

"I usually wear an 'M' size."

"Okay." He said and walked back to his closet. He picked out a bright blue shirt and low-waist jeans. He folded them and put them on the left side of the bathroom door. He knocked and said, "I have put your clothes on *your* right side outside the bathroom door. I'll not be looking so don't worry."

"Okay."

He took the towel off his waist and started to wipe himself. Once done, he threw the towel on that same pile on the right side of the door. Then he took out a light green t-shirt and a black pyjama and put them on. He looked at his window. The rain had gotten fierce and the drops were hitting the window harder. The room only had two voices, the shower drops and the rain drops. All the time spent in the shower had caused him to find music in random sounds. And he was feeling a tune amidst the combination of the rain drops and shower drops.

He listened to the tune for a while. The hitting of the drops on the window was surprisingly in sync with the drops in the shower. The tune was familiar. It was an old song. He first hummed the tune of the song. But the song seemed somewhat incomplete. He needed a partner— a female partner. He thought of asking Chanda but immediately dismissed the thought. He sat at the edge of the bed and started to sway forward and backward, as if sitting on an invisible rocking chair.

After swaying for a few seconds, he grew restless. He sat straight and inhaled deeply. Then he cleared his throat and started to sing.

Bheegi-bheegi raaton mein,

Meethi-meethi baaton mein,

Aisi barsaaton mein, kaisa lagta hai?

Suddenly out of the blue, another voice boomed in the room, chiming in and matching the rhythm and continuing the song.

Aisa lagta hai, Tum banke baadal,

Mere badan ko, bhigoke mohe,

Chhed rahe ho, chhed rahe ho.

Shantanu turned towards the voice with surprise and disbelief. The voice had come from the shower. He at first stared at the bathroom door. He was waiting for Chanda to pop her head out and ask about the girl singing. But when none of that happened, he asked to the gate carefully, "Was that you?"

"Yes. Who else?" Chanda replied.

"Nothing. I was just surprised that you know this song and that you can sing so well."

"Thank you. I used to sing when I was little."

"Impressive."

"I know."

"Then why did you stop singing?"

"I just got busy; like all the people."

Before he could say something, the door of the shower opened a little and a hand poked out and started to tap at the ground blindly. After three or four taps, the hand rested on the clothes that were put there. The hand grabbed the clothes and took them inside. After a few moments, Chanda came out with the towel wrapped around her head. The second towel was resting on her forearm like a waiter's napkin. She asked where she should put the towel. He pointed to the pile of clothes. Chanda cringed and threw the towel on the pile. Then she bent towards her right and opened the twisted part of the towel and started to wipe her hair.

Shantanu was looking at her intently. Her wet hairs were shining in the fluorescent light. She was looking at some point distant, possibly outside of the room. Her hands were rubbing her hairs with the towel and he was looking at her as if she was the only person in the world. It must've been approximately two minutes when she noticed his eyes on her. She looked at him back and raised her eyebrows asking what happened. He still looked at her unchanged. She snapped her fingers and he was pulled out of his trance. He blinked as if he had just woken up from a dream.

"What are you looking at?" Chanda asked.

"Nothing… just your hair."

Chanda smiled internally at this lame cover-up response. Even though Chanda knew Shantanu since 8th class, he was still acting as if he was on a first date. She said teasing him, "What about them?"

Shantanu was not ready for such question. For a moment, he was speechless. Then, somehow finding the words, he spoke, "They're beautiful."

It was Chanda's turn to be surprised. She had not expected such answer. She just smiled in reply and kept on drying her hair. The conversation between them seemed telepathic. Whatever Chanda wanted, Shantanu seemed to instantly acknowledge and put the thought into action. Until Chayansh arrived, he and Chanda spent the time sitting opposite to each other on the same bed, without uttering a single word to each other. With some people you share your thoughts, with some you share yourself, but there are only a few people in the world that you can share your silence. Even if Shantanu didn't love Chanda, he had a connection with her that went beyond anything physical or mental.

One thing that both of them didn't know was that around the same time that they reached the hostel, Poorna had slumped on the bed thinking about the worst date she ever had.

XV

After Shantanu and Chanda had left, Poorna waited for a little while. During that time, she ate the pasta. After eating, she felt hungrier, so she ate the second plate of pasta as well. She ordered another plate. Waiter got busy with the order and she waited. After ten minutes, she heard the rain outside. She texted Fareed.

The reply came another five minutes later. It said that he was just five minutes away with a smiley. The smiley brought a slight smile on her face. She held her face in her hands and started to wait again. The restaurant had the sole customer, her. After five minutes, her order was right in front of her but her boyfriend wasn't. She again texted him. The same reply came back. When the dish got cold, she again texted him. He replied that he couldn't come because there had been a flooding in the way and the path was blocked. She didn't believe him, but she had no choice other than to believe whatever he said.

She got up and went to the counter. She asked what the total was. The cashier said, "The total is 180 rupees." She reached in her purse.

"That won't be necessary." A voice came from her right. She looked in the direction. A person dressed in a light green shirt and black jeans. The colour had changed since the person was drenched. He had recently got a haircut which was spoilt now. He had a smile that showed that he was glad to have come at the right time. Her face started to glow with a smile as she exclaimed, "Fari!" and hugged him. He parted her instantly saying, "Move, I'm wet."

"But you said you weren't coming." She said after breaking the hug.

"Well, I wanted to surprise you. But now that I'm here, I realize that it was a stupid plan."

"Stupid indeed." She said chuckling.

She held his hand and pulled him inside. When she did that, another person entered the restaurant. This person was wearing red T-shirt and blue pants along with white sneakers. He, too, was drenched. His hairs were longer than Fareed's and because of his T-shirt clinging to his body; one would say that the guy was muscular, probably more muscular than Fareed. As Poorna and Fareed sat on the table next to each other, that guy sat right next to her. She first looked at the guy and then looked at Fareed, demanding an explanation.

"Poorna, meet my batchmate, Anikesh; and Anikesh, this is Poorna." Anikesh forwarded his hand which Poorna shook reluctantly. She was disappointed that Fareed brought someone else to their date. The date went only one-sided. It looked like only Poorna had thought of this as a date, while Fareed had decided to make it a get-together. The conversation continued only between Fareed and Anikesh, that too about the courses, exams, scope, college admissions, etc. She was obviously bored. Two minutes into the conversation, suddenly Anikesh's phone rang. From what she heard, she deduced that some friend was asking about their whereabouts and just like that, Anikesh had invited this friend to village 69.

After what seemed like five minutes, the friend entered village 69. What shocked Poorna was when the friend sat down and told them that others were on their way. She asked in disbelief, "What others?"

"Well, some of the friends are also coming." Fareed replied.

"What for?" She sounded so rude that it surprised herself.

"Well, as you know, we never meet anywhere else other than classroom. So, we thought that it would be good to have a reunion."

A reunion is supposed to happen between old classmates, not current batch mates. She thought. Then she got up and started to leave without saying a word. At the entry, Fareed stopped her and said, "Why are you leaving?"

Because you ruined our date with a reunion. "Nothing; I'm just not feeling well."

"Would you be able to go by yourself?"

"Yes, yes."

"Oh, and one more thing."

"What?"

"Can you pay the bill this time? I forgot to bring any money."

You've brought money, all right. You just need it to contribute in the group party that you all are going to have. Just say it straight, Fari. "No problem." She said and paid the bill of 180 rupees and went straight outside.

Outside, it was still raining but she didn't care. Why should she care if her own boyfriend doesn't care about her getting wet? She descended the steps and just as absent-mindedly walked out of the street and hailed an auto-rickshaw. The auto-rickshaw driver proposed a fare that was completely and clearly unrealistic, but she didn't argue or negotiated. The auto-rickshaw driver dropped her off and then she went in the A & A girls' hostel.

Just as absent minded, she walked up to room no. 306 and firstly took a shower with her clothes on and then took off her clothes in the shower itself. Pictures of rains in their farms started to form up before her closed eyes. It had been so long since she had remembered her home. On any normal day, she would consciously dismiss the images but today she let them flow through her mind.

The farm looked happy when the rain commenced. Before the rains, there were winds howling throughout the land. The shed that she and her father had recently built looked like it was about to uproot. Her father held two of the supporting beams and told Poorna to keep off. But Poorna being Poorna, she couldn't just stand there. So, she ran and grabbed hold of one beam by wrapping her arms around it in a hug. Her father smiled at first at Poorna's effort, but then asked her again to keep off as it was dangerous. When she refused to move, her father told her to hold his leg to prevent him from flying. It was a cute and simple little trick that worked perfectly on her. She left the beam and held on to her father's right leg. The winds started to grow in intensity. She could see the nerves bulging out of her father's hands. She was marveled at the strength her father had. From her view, it looked like an epic battle between a god and a human. Finally, her father had to give in to nature's forces. He let go of the beams and quickly wrapped his arms around her to safeguard her from the beams that were going around randomly in the wind. While her father looked worried, Poorna felt tranquil. She didn't know why her father was wrapping himself around her, so she pegged it to be a hug and hugged him back. She was happy feeling the warmth of her father's arms. The storm, the winds, the season, none of it mattered. She wasn't scared of anything. That was when the rain started. The drops hit her small and mushy face rather hard but she was soon carried by her father to their home where he dried her himself and then put her down on the bed and sang a song in Punjabi until she slept. She didn't remember the words perfectly but the tune and melody of it still remained. Her father's voice was the most melodious one she had ever heard.

That's the one thing that she could never forget.

When Poorna opened her eyes, she felt a lump in her throat. She noticed that she had sat with her knees folded that were now touching her breasts. Her eyes felt hot and so did her cheeks. Her head felt heavy and her ears were ringing. Even the sweetest memory pains when you know it is never going to happen again.

Poorna missed her father terribly. She folded her knees more and put her head between them. For the first time since her father's death, she cried. She cried in the shower for about ten minutes incessantly. She got up sobbing, washed her face in the shower and then turned the knob and stepped out. She pulled out a towel from her cupboard and wiped herself. Even wiping herself felt like heavy work. When the weight of emotions is put down, we are left with the weight of emptiness. When she was done, she left the towel on the ground and slumped on the bed, stark naked. Outside, the sound of rain drops felt like tiny stones thrown at the window. Depressed under the weight of her own emptiness, she quickly fell asleep.

XVI

The next morning when she woke up, it was 11:23 A.M. She couldn't believe that she had slept for almost 13 hours. She initially thought about the classes she missed, but soon she realized that today was Sunday. Even though she was very well awake, she didn't feel like getting up from the bed. She turned many times in the bed, hoping that she would sleep. But sleep was elusive to her.

Finally fed up from the waiting, she got up and went to the toilet first. After getting her teeth brushed, she looked at the time. It was 11:45 A.M. It was the fastest she had ever gotten ready. She sat on the bed, not waiting for the clock to strike 12:00, but wondering what she would do when she will have to face the boy, or more likely the boy's voice. It had been almost three months that they had been singing together, but both of them didn't know the names of each other, only the voices of their singing. That was what they both found convenient. And it had been going on good.

She unlocked her phone, and logged in to her Facebook. She first checked the friend requests section. She had 345 requests pending. It wasn't that she wasn't active on Facebook, but since she and Fareed had gotten into a relationship, she used to surf on Facebook through his ID. That habit had caused her to use her own ID less and less. She scrolled down the requests and accepted the requests of the people she knew and left all the others like that. Still, even after accepting so many requests, she had 298 requests pending. She grimaced at how people get so much time to send friend requests to unknown people. Was everyone in the world suddenly desperate for friends?

She logged out and locked the phone and threw it on the bed. She looked at the clock. It was 11:57 A.M. She got up and walked to the cupboard. She opened it and produced a towel. Holding the towel in her underarm, she walked to the shower. She didn't want to, but she had become used to it. *Another habit of mine set up by someone else,* she thought and went inside.

She hung her towel on the bar behind her and waited for a sound of door opening. After three minutes, she heard the sound of the opening of the door of the other side. She heard the boy humming something, but she didn't care. She was determined not to sing today.

Just like every day, she heard the daily question.

"So, what do you want to sing today?"

If it would've been some other day, Poorna would've started to sing, hoping that the boy on the other side will pick up, which he did so many times that it was almost like he knew all the songs that she could possibly sing. But today was different, so the reply came back harsh.

"I don't want to sing today."

Silence. She waited for a sound.

"…But why? What happened?" the reply came after a whole minute.

The question further irritated Poorna. *Yesterday Fari and now him. What is wrong with guys? Why can't they just leave a girl to her own thoughts?* She thought and replied, "Nothing. I just don't want to sing."

She had expected Shantanu to give up. As much as she had seen in life, boys are lazy when it comes to trying once more. There was silence on the other end for a while. When Poorna thought that he had finally given up, she turned the shower knob. Just as the water began cascading down her already naked body, she heard a whistle. It wasn't just ordinary whistling, it was a tune. He was whistling a tune. Then she heard him take an *Aalaap.* Then with the precise highs and lows, the song began.

Yeh sham mastani,

Madhosh kiye jaaye,

Mujhe dor koi kheeche,

Teri ore liye jaaye.

Yeh sham mastani,

Madhosh kiye jaaye,

Mujhe dor koi kheeche,

Teri ore liye jaaye.

Shantanu started to sing the interlude. Meanwhile, Poorna rolled her eyes. She hated it when things didn't go according to her. He was singing the Kishore Kumar hit with ambient dexterity.

Door rahti hai tu,

Mere paas aati nahi,

Hoton pe tere,

Kabhi pyaas aati nahi,

Aisa lage, jaise ki tu,

Haske, zehar koi piye jaaye;

Yeh sham mastani,

Madhosh kiye jaaye,

Mujhe dor koi kheeche,

Teri ore liye jaaye.

While Shantanu was singing, Poorna was trying not to get affected by the song. She knew that if he could make her shiver with his songs, then he can very well change her mood in a snap. She was resisting on the outside, but somewhere in the back of her mind, she was feeling special on his effort to lift her mood. Then she heard the song being continued.

Baat jab main karoon,

Mujhe rok deti hai kyun,

Teri neechi nazar,

Mujhe tok deti hai kyun,

Teri haya, teri sharam,

Teri kasam, mere hoth siye jaaye;

Yeh sham mastani,

Madhosh kiye jaaye,

Mujhe dor koi kheeche,

Teri ore liye jaaye.

Poorna could sense movement in her feet. All her deceit had vanished, but for some reason, she was still resisting. She didn't want to make it easy for him. The song felt exactly as if he was trying to convince her. It made her feel thrilled. She was smiling slightly now, enjoying the ecstatic position of the person being coaxed. Meanwhile, the song continued.

Ek roothi hui,

Taqdeer jaise koi,

Khaamosh aise hai tu,

Tasveer jaise koi,

Teri nazar, banke zubaan,

Lekin tere, paigaam diye jaaye;

Yeh sham mastani,

Madhosh kiye jaaye,

Mujhe dor koi kheeche,

Teri ore liye jaaye.

Yeh sham mastani,

Madhosh kiye jaaye,

Mujhe dor koi kheeche,

Teri ore liye jaaye.

The whistle began again with the same tune. Poorna was enjoying the song fully now. When the whistle began, she started to whistle in sync.

Both of them— while whistling the song with the same tune— felt exactly the same. They felt the connection to each other deeper than ever. They felt the shivers down their spine simply by the sync of their voices. They felt that they were only the person that they actually were, not some image they had created. They felt the closeness to each other while being separated by a wall approximately 4 inches thick. They felt the need of being with each other, no matter how impossible it sounded.

For the first time, they felt *love.*

XVII

"I have a question to ask you." Shantanu's voice boomed in Poorna's ear after five days from her date fiasco. Both were done 'shower singing' and now were wiping themselves. She kept wiping her body and replied, "What question?"

"It's something about girls."

The sentence immediately struck on one cause in Poorna's mind. She knew that many boys are literally unaware of periods and some are even afraid of this natural process. She thought that the boy must've seen something. She immediately went into sympathetic mode. Her voice reached an amazing low and politeness that even she was unaware of.

"Don't worry, it's all right. It's just a natural process."

On the other side, Shantanu was confused from this sudden change of tone from the girl. Why this girl suddenly sounded like a sympathetic nurse? He asked, "What happened? Why are you talking like that?"

"Like what?" the tone had only grown more sympathetic.

"Like some relative of mine is admitted in a hospital."

"Well, the matter is somewhat serious, right?"

"No! I just want to ask a question."

"I know what it is about."

"You do?"

"Yes."

"Then pray tell me."

"It's about… um… 'That time of the month', right?"

"What? No."

"No?"

"No."

"Fine, then. Ask your question." Her voice returned to normal.

There was momentary silence in the shower. She waited. After two seconds, the question echoed in the shower.

"Have you ever been loved by someone you can never love back?"

"It's called friend-zoning."

"No, it's not friend-zone."

"You know you're saying that to a girl, right?"

"Fine. It is about friend-zoning." The reply came after a few seconds.

"That's a good boy. Now tell me what happened."

Shantanu narrated all the incidents with proper editing. He was careful about giving out the name of Chanda to her. He thought of girls as some kind of super detectives who can find any person better than the police itself. He changed the name to Chandrika. Poorna listened intently and kept giving reactions and asked questions in between to catch up. When he was done, he took a deep breath. He waited for a sound.

“Well, as far as I’m concerned, you’re doing wrong to Chandrika.”

“Please tell me something I don’t know already.”

“Well, this is the most complicated type of relations.”

“Obviously.”

“Well, I do have a solution to this but…” she stopped mid-sentence.

“...But what?”

“…but I don’t think you’ll be able to do it.”

“At least tell me what the solution is.”

“Well, just confess everything to her and then tell her that you still want to be friends, if that is something that’s possible.”

“What?” Shantanu was shocked.

“Listen, it’s the only way.”

“No, I can’t do it.”

“Well, then, you would have to carry it on just as messed up as it already is.”

“Come on, isn’t there any other way?”

“Well, the pain in this relation is inevitable, but you can maybe reduce it to some extent.”

“How?” There was hope in his voice.

“‘Love flings’.”

“What?”

"'Love flings'."

"I get that. But I meant what does 'Love flings' mean?"

Poorna took a deep breath. She had been waiting for this moment since the time she had coined the term. With a smile on her face, she started, "Ok, then, listen carefully. It happens more than often that a guy falls for us girls but we girls, we see the guy as a good friend. And honestly, I see no fault in it. You can't force someone to love you. So, the guy ends up in a place where he tries to be more than a friend but can't. It's a place popularly called 'friend-zone'.

So, you must've seen in films, or possibly must've experienced this yourself, that when the guy does something cute or self-less— or even when he does nothing of that sorts— we girls give him small tokens of our appreciation, which is usually seen as a girl giving the guy false hope. Instead, I call them 'Love flings'.

'Love flings' are basically momentary slips in a girl's mind where we feel so adorned by the guy's attempts that we actually forget that he's a guy. Yes, that happens. We forget that our friend is a guy who only hopes to score and doesn't know shit about being a girl's friend. We treat him like we would treat any dear friend and perform a few small acts of romance, like kisses on the cheek or hugs, or in some special cases, kisses on the lips. But the only bitch about this situation is that it is only momentary. And just like many other momentary things, it goes just as fast as it comes. So, it ends on a weird note. It ends with the guy feeling euphoric and hopeful and the girl feeling confused about what to do with the situation she had just created. And that's 'Love flings' for you."

After this prolonged lecture, Shantanu felt heaviness in the head. It was an information overload for his mind. He was trying to soak it all in and relate it to his situation. But she was a bit worried on his silence. She called out to him, "Are you still here?"

"Uh... yes. Yes, I am."

"Are you okay?"

"I'm not sure."

"So, was this helpful?"

"Oh, it was so helpful that I think a book should be written about it."

Poorna's small laugh was the only response.

XVIII

A week after that, Shantanu was invited to Chayansh's house party. It was his parents' marriage anniversary. When he arrived at Chayansh's home, he found the room to be rather dark. He went inside and called out to Chayansh, but no answer came. He held on to the card under his arm and started to look for a switch. Suddenly the lights turned on and people materialized in front of him and everybody yelled, "Surprise!"

Like the word itself, Shantanu's face had a look of surprise as well. Everyone was huddled around him and saying something all at once which made it undetectable as to what even one of them was saying. Chayansh pushed his way through and hugged a confused and wonderstruck Shantanu. He pulled the card out from his underarm and hugged him back, confused. Chayansh patted his back and practically yelled in his ear, "So how do you like the arrangement?"

Shantanu looked around. The walls had been decorated with Christmas lights. The same ones were used to make a chandelier on the ceiling. The lights gave the room a light hue. To Him, it gave out the look of a rave party. He looked around to his right. He saw Chayansh's dad's bar decorated with expensive spirits. He was surprised because the bar usually remained empty. Chayansh's dad had quit alcohol three years ago. He only kept a few bottles as a collection, which consisted of only super-expensive liquors.

Chayansh broke the hug and looked at him expectantly. Shantanu forced a smile and yelled, "It's amazing." Chayansh yelled, "Yo, DJ, blast away."

Everyone turned in the direction he yelled towards. Shantanu saw that a DJ was set up in one corner of the room. A young man who looked like he was in his twenties put headphones on his ears and started to adjust some dials and the music started to play through the speakers around the DJ himself. A remix started to play. It contained one or two lines from the old songs with the mash up of bass and treble and EDM. Every time the song changed, the tune and the levels of bass changed as well. Most of the songs that were being played were the ones that he listened to. Everyone started to dance with the lyrics of the evergreen songs, while he looked around himself confused like a man in a strange land. He was the only one standing still in the middle of a dancing crowd. He looked like someone in a party song video.

Why is this place decorated like it's a fucking rave party? And where the hell are aunty and uncle? It is their anniversary, right?

Shantanu was puzzled by these questions when he felt someone tugging at his arm. He turned towards his right and found that it was Chanda tugging at his arm. He gestured a 'what?' with his head, to which she replied by pulling his arm gently, indicating to come with her. He left the card on a nearby sofa and followed her.

With her leading the way, he crossed the hall where the party was being held, and headed towards the stairs. Chayansh's and Chanda's house was a three-storied mansion looking bungalow. It had a porch, a balcony, a terrace big enough to be played cricket on, a garden with sizeable number of flowers and creepers and multiple stairways for each floor. Chayansh, Chanda, Shantanu and their other friends used these multiple stairways to play games like hide-and-seek, chor-police, etc. when they were still children.

Shantanu knew from his experience that while there are multiple stairways for each floor, there is only one stairway for terrace, and the staircase they were heading towards led to terrace. On the way, he saw two people sitting on the stairs. The two of them looked like they were talking. Chanda and he soon found out that it was Alfaz and Sarthi from their coaching institute, Allen.

Alfaz was from the engineering stream while Sarthi was from biological stream. It was surely an unlikely match, but a match nevertheless. Shantanu smiled at the talking couple and looking at Chanda, he thought that she must be smiling too. She walked ahead and he followed suit. She stood right in front of them. It took a few seconds for Alfaz and Sarthi to notice their presence. For a moment, all four of them fell silent. The looks on Alfaz and Sarthi's faces were like those children who had been caught fighting.

"If you guys want to talk, there are other staircases to sit on, but personally I would prefer that you guys get a room." Chanda said with a wink.

"We were just talking." Sarthi justified unnecessarily.

"I can see that, genius. But I'm just saying that you should be talking somewhere more private, like a room."

"Where were you going with him anyway?" Alfaz tried to shift the focus to Shantanu.

"She was helping me find you so that Chayansh could get his money back that he lent you a week ago." He chimed in.

Alfaz went red in the face with the mention of the loan.

"But…" He paused for a better attention span.

"I can say to Chayansh that I couldn't find you if you follow the advice of this lovely lady here." He gestured towards Chanda who smiled at this mafia-type gentleness. She started to tell them.

"Go downstairs and turn a left. On your right, you'll find a room that is equipped with a queen size bed along with lights with adjustable brightness. The room also has an attached bathroom-toilet. The room has a self-locking mechanism which activates only when you insert a card that you will find hanging behind the door itself. Use it if you want further privacy. What's more, the room has an automatic AC that can sense human presence and directs the air flow accordingly. I think that should make your day, or should I say night?"

Both Alfaz and Sarthi were confused. Both of them first looked at Chanda and Shantanu who had sly smiles on their faces then looked at each other. Silently, they both got up and went downstairs. Chanda started to walk up the stairs and Shantanu followed. He turned to look at the departing couple and saw that they were holding hands before they turned left. He smiled and walked with Chanda.

At the top of the stairs, she opened a door to her right. She stepped out and he followed as usual. Outside, it took less than a second for him to recognize why he was brought upstairs. As he looked around the terrace, he saw candles arranged in the shape of a smile. He knew that he should've smiled but somehow he couldn't. He was nervous. Chanda left him standing there and went back to close the terrace gate. He was transfixed on the candles, wondering what the occasion was because he was now sure that it wasn't uncle and auntie's marriage anniversary.

"How do you like it?" She whispered in his ear.

Chanda's breath on his skin made his mind go blank. He felt shivers on his whole body. Shantanu didn't come to reality until he felt Chanda's hand creeping under his arm. She slowly traced her way to his fingers and intertwined her fingers with his. He looked down at their interlocked fingers and then at Chanda who was looking towards him with a twinkle in her eyes. Her eyes felt powerful, as if they were radiating a glow that he couldn't handle. He looked away and replied, "It's very creative."

"So you like it?"

"Yes, but..."

"What?"

"What's the occasion?"

"What?" For a moment, she felt she didn't hear him correctly.

"I'm asking what the occasion is. Surely, it isn't your mom and dad's marriage anniversary."

"So you're saying that you don't know what the occasion is."

"I'm sorry. I think I forgot." He feared he had forgotten something important.

Chanda stood in front of him and stared at him. It felt like she was inspecting something. She looked at him from head to feet and then took a deep sigh. Shantanu became more nervous. She took two steps ahead and hugged him. He was confused. All he did was hug her back. After two seconds, she whispered in his ear, "Happy birthday, Shantu."

XIX

For a moment, Shantanu couldn't believe Chanda. He dug his hand into his pocket and took out his phone. He unlocked it and checked the date. 6th December, 2018. Of course, it was his birthday. When he was putting his phone back in his pocket, Chanda gave him a kiss on the cheek and hugged him tighter. That froze him right there, as it usually did.

"I have never seen someone forget their own birthday."

He gave out a little laugh in response.

"Doesn't anybody call you or whatsapp you on your birthday?" She joked.

Shantanu's smile disappeared. Chanda may have joked to make the mood a little lighter, but it struck a chord of hurt inside him. He broke the hug and sat on the parapet. She didn't understand the sudden change of mood. For the first time, He actually looked sad to Chanda. Somehow, it worried her. She sat close to him on the parapet. This part of parapet on the house was around three feet in height and was the seat of Excellency when Chayansh, Chanda and Shantanu were kids. It was the seat of Excellency because it was the only location on the terrace devoid of the creepers. It was a place where you can actually sit and look out over the city without destroying the soft tendrils of the creepers.

"I'm sorry." Chanda said after a minute of silence.

"No, no. It's not your fault."

"But what happened? Why do you suddenly sound so... sad?"

"It's nothing. It's... nothing."

Shantanu looked to the city in front of him while Chanda kept staring at him. She had never seen such dread on his face. She slid herself closer to him, their arms were now touching. She took his hand in hers and said, "You can tell me what's bothering you."

Shantanu turned to look at her. Her head was bowed down. This time he noticed what she was wearing. She was wearing an Egyptian blue, button-down collared shirt along with white skinny jeans. She was wearing her hair open and she had long earrings along with a small nose pin. She was the personification of perfection. He felt like he should click a picture of her. He nudged Chanda a little and said, "You want to know how you made me sad?"

She nodded in a yes.

"Okay, you know that my parents died when I was eight, right?"

She again nodded.

"Well, after their death, it was a really controversial matter on who will take me in. Somehow, all the people who told me that children are gifts of god were suddenly reluctant to take care of one. So, for a month, I was left in an orphanage. In the meantime, my relatives had left the decision of my custody in the hands of court. For the time being, I was made to quit school, tuitions and all the things only a guardian would provide for. The kids were okay at the orphanage, so was the caretaker, but I missed the tranquility I felt at my home. You know that there are approximately 6 lakh cases pending in various high courts of India for more than a decade? How could it have been possible that my little case could make it any faster? So, as a result, there were delays. My orphanage stay was extended from a month to a whole year. In the orphanage, I started to detest my relatives. I mean, even if they didn't want me, the least they could've done was to visit me a few times. I was in the need of even an illusion of love.

After another three months, the verdict finally came out and the court had decided that I would be put in the custody of my *chacha* and *chachi* as they were the closest of kin to my late father. If this would've been a film, I would be happy by the news and we would be a happy family... but life only coincides with films when films are actually based on a true story. It wasn't that they didn't care for me or that they were always trying to get rid of me, but they only cared for me like a liability. Otherwise, they didn't care if I'm studying or not, if I'm happy or not... if I'm depressed or not..." Shantanu paused and took a deep breath.

Chanda was listening with the utmost shock she ever experienced in her life. Whatever Shantanu was telling her was hard to believe considering the type of experiences she had with him. In their group, he was the most carefree, energetic and happy-go-lucky person. Nothing ever troubled him. He was the one who told them that the things that they worry about so much right now wouldn't mean anything to them later in life. He basically taught them the concept of enjoying life. The fact that someone with that kind of history could be like the Shantanu she knew was hard to digest for her.

After the pause, he continued, "So, I joined the school from the class I dropped out of. Obviously, I had no friends of any sorts up until 6th class. They were all very younger than me. In 6th class, I overheard a conversation between two students discussing life at their respective coaching institutes. That was when I knew that these institutes take up coaching as early as 6th class. So, I decided to enroll. My foster parents didn't even bat an eye about my admission. They just handed me an ATM card to pull the required money out and said a formal 'best of luck'. I had to sign myself under the guardian signature space. I was depressed. I was lonely. I was the exact opposite of what you know of me now. Back then, you wouldn't be wrong if you termed me as 'suicidal' ..."

Shantanu's voice had started to turn hoarse. Chanda could see that his eyes had started to well up. He blinked hard and took a deep breath and controlled himself. Once he was successful in fighting back the tears, he continued, "So I packed my bags, took out some money I thought would be required to buy some stuff for the room and came here and took admission in 7th class. The only thing I left behind at that place was my old self. I was determined to make friends, to be able to laugh and smile again, to have fun, to be carefree, to be able to love someone again, but most of all; I was determined to be happy again. And the rest is history."

Shantanu turned to look at Chanda. He saw that she was crying. He didn't know why, but it immediately worried him. He cupped her face in his hands and wiped the tears off her face with his thumbs. Some of the mascara had trickled down her cheeks along with the tears. He put one hand in his back pocket and produced a handkerchief.

He usually didn't keep handkerchief on himself. He had started this habit recently because one day the girl on the other side had told him that a man who carries a handkerchief is considered elegant and sophisticated and that girls loved a gentleman. On that day, he bought a bunch of handkerchiefs and put one in each of his pants so that he won't forget. That habit had been remained unused until now.

He used one side of the folded handkerchief and gently dabbed the handkerchief where the mascara had come down. Once he was done dabbing, he gently wiped the mascara off her cheeks and dabbed again a little under her eyes. All the while his left hand cupped Chanda's face and she kept looking at him like she was seeking for something in Shantanu's face. Once done, he put the handkerchief back in his pocket. He cupped her face with both hands again and smiled with affection. He said in a voice so low that it was almost a whisper, "Please don't cry again. It makes my heart sink."

Their faces were only centimeters away. Chanda could feel Shantanu's breath on her lips. His breath smelled of peppermint. A mouth spray, same as hers. The proximity between him and her *and* his touch gave her goose bumps with electricity through the body as usual but this time, it made her heart accelerate. She felt like her heart was thumping so fast that its beats were not only audible to her but to him as well.

She didn't know when she leaned forward. It was almost involuntary. It felt as if she was a piece of iron being attracted towards a powerful magnet. The movement was slow, but it felt slower to Shantanu. He himself felt drawing towards her. This time he didn't resist. He let go of himself because this time he wanted to let go.

First, their heads touched. They could feel each other's breath. Both their breaths smelled of peppermint. Then slowly he felt Chanda's face tilting towards his left. Almost involuntarily, he tilted his face to his right. Both were anxious. Both were scared. Both were excited. Both of them closed their eyes. Both of them felt each other's lips graze against each other's lips. For a moment, both stopped moving. The touch of her lips was incredibly soft. He could tell that even with the lipstick on her lips. He felt that he should have applied some kind of cream to his lips because he knew his lips were a disaster. On the other hand, Chanda thought of his lips as interesting. She was a bit astonished with the tingles his lips made her feel.

That was when it happened. Chanda started to suck on his lower lip and he reciprocated. Both of them exchanged their breaths. He turned 90 degrees and spread his legs so that his one leg was on the terrace and one was hanging from the parapet. In response, she slid a little and sat in the space between his legs and wrapped her legs around his waist and her arms around his head. Even they didn't know how long their passionate kiss lasted.

XX

It took more than an hour of dancing for Chayansh to realize that Shantanu wasn't around him. It actually took the finishing of the bottle of Old Monk he was holding in his hand and was occasionally drinking from it neat in the middle of the dance. He was already feeling light, swaying to the shaking of his own legs rather than the music. And he wasn't alone in that, almost everyone in the party was drunk-dancing, except for the DJ.

Chayansh knew why Shantanu would have vanished from the party. He knew that Shantanu didn't drink. He actively avoided parties where most of the crowd consisted of habitual drinkers.

Although both Chanda and Chayansh were allowed to and used to drink often, he was the sober friend who dropped both of them home. Chayansh had a noble idea on one of those trips of making him drink something alcoholic on his 18th birthday. As soon as the thought crossed his mind, he was more than determined to find Shantanu. He ran to the bar, tripped three times along the way on thin air. He picked himself up with the aid of the bar counter and told the bartender to hand him a bottle of chilled beer.

With a chilled beer in his hand and a fabulous idea in his mind, Chayansh started to roam around the house at his own pace, often bumping into people and inanimate objects and apologizing. Finally, he decided that maybe Shantanu was on the roof, so he started to climb the staircase that lead to the terrace. When he had climbed 4/5th of the stairs, he saw the terrace gate open and Chanda coming out along with Shantanu. Seeing him, Chayansh became anxiously excited about getting him drunk. He hurled himself towards Shantanu and hugged him as tight as he could without breaking the beer bottle in his hand.

"Happy birthday, Shantu."

"Thanks, man. What is that smell?"

"Don't worry, he's just drunk." Chanda said in her matter-of-fact tone.

"Probably Old Monk this time, am I right, buddy?"

"You are right as rain." Chayansh said slurring.

"What are you doing up here, man?"

"Question is: what are you doing?"

Shantanu and Chanda looked at each other in question.

"It's your 18th birthday, Shantu, not a dry day." He danced the beer bottle in front of Shantanu.

"No, bro, I told you I don't drink."

"Drink this for my love, bro." Chayansh put a hand on the back of his head and started to push his head to the beer bottle.

"Chanda, please." He looked pleadingly at Chanda.

"I think it's about time you started drinking, Shantu." His eyes widened with surprise on Chanda's response.

"Drink it already." Chayansh had brought his lips only centimeters away from the bottle.

Shantanu knew that it was now or never. He closed his eyes and blindly pushed Chayansh. It wasn't hard pushing him, since he was already tipsy enough. The only problem was that they were facing the stairs. His senses were already clogged with effects of alcohol and so was his balance, so when Shantanu pushed him, he fell down the stairs without resistance. He fell and rolled and twisted and hit himself in many places but he only stopped when he reached the bottom. Meanwhile, Shantanu and Chanda ran downstairs as fast as they could without falling.

The party was still in its mood. Everyone was enjoying even if drunk or not. People were gathered in the middle under the chandelier dancing to the beats of evergreen songs with a new touch of remix. The song that was being currently played was 'Babuji dheere chalna' from the film 'Aar-Paar'. When Shantanu reached the bottom of the stairs, he saw that hardly any people had noticed Chayansh and those who did, ignored him thinking he fell because he was drunk. There was some logic to that thought. Everyone tends to think that helping someone is only appropriate when they ask to be helped. A drunken man can cut his own wrist but still won't ask for even a band-aid.

Shantanu sat right beside Chayansh and turned him over so that he would lie on his back. He took his head in his lap and started to shake him calling his name repetitively.

"I think he's passed out." He said when Chayansh didn't come to consciousness. He grabbed his one arm and asked Chanda to lift the other one. They both put each arm over their shoulder and held it with the other hand. They used the free hand to put under his legs and lifted him with both their arms supporting him. They found him heavy for someone to be considered underweight in his class.

With slow and measured steps, they both were able to transport Chayansh to the nearby sofa. They first sat him and then made him lie on his back. They both took out their phones and put them on the table right in front of the sofa as the phones in their pockets had started to dig into their skins of their pelvic region. Shantanu and Chanda catch their breath for a few seconds, and then he said, "We have to shut this party down."

"Why?"

"Because that's enough for one night."

"What's enough?"

"...this drunk drama." He pointed at passed out Chayansh.

Chanda looked at her passed out brother. She could see little cuts and nicks on his face and the parts of his arms that were exposed. His hairs were a mess and she was pretty sure that the stain on his shoes wasn't some kind of oil paint. She felt disgusted of him. For the first time in her life, she was disgusted by her drunken brother. Maybe it was because she was sober. Usually she was so drunk out of her mind to even remember the things she did until Shantanu told her the next day. She took a deep breath and nodded her head in a yes.

"Well, then, what are you waiting for?"

"What?"

"Go ahead and tell everyone to get out. Tell them that party's over."

"Why?"

"...Because it is your house."

"But this is *your* birthday party."

"Since it is your house, you have the authority over it. You and Chayansh are the ones who can invite people or make them go."

Chanda looked at the crowd dancing under the chandelier. Then she took a look at the people distributed around in various corners of the house. Her mind labeled it as an impossible task just to say everyone to get out, let alone escort them out.

"Still... I think since this is your birthday party, you should call the shots." She said shrugging.

Shantanu sighed and started to walk towards the dancing crowd. Just when Shantanu started to go through the crowd, someone put a hand on Chanda's shoulder.

XXI

Chanda turned to see that *someone* was Poorna. Chanda and Poorna hugged each other and the first question she asked was, "So, how did it go?"

The question made Chanda remember of what happened on the rooftop. She felt shy. She could feel the blood rushing to her cheeks. The result of her plan was more than she had expected. In response to Poorna's question, she just bowed her head a little and started to play with her fingers. She smiled at Chanda's response. She bent her knees a little and looked up at Chanda's face. She was blushing like never before. Poorna smiled fully and cupped her face and asked again, "My blushing angel, please tell me how did it go."

Truth to be told, Chanda didn't want to tell Poorna about her and Shantanu's kiss. In fact, she didn't want to tell anybody, not even Sonia. She wanted it to be only between her and him. She wanted to hold on to this memory. Sharing it seemed like giving it away. She didn't want to give away what she considered her sweetest memory. But she knew that she had to tell Poorna. She was entitled to know about everything. After all, it was her plan.

"Let's just say that the outcome was way better than both of us expected."

Chanda's words spiked the curiosity and happiness inside Poorna. Something good had happened. And if the result was better than a hug, then surely it was worth knowing.

"Come on, tell me what happened. I'm dying to know."

"Well..." Chanda was about to tell Poorna about the kiss when the music stopped all of a sudden. She and Poorna looked at the DJ like everyone else. They saw that Shantanu was fumbling with the cordless mic at the DJ table. While the DJ was helping him with the mic, the whole crowd started to boo him. He finally managed to turn the mic on. He first checked the voice with a few taps on the mic, and then his voice boomed across the house.

"I'm sorry to disturb you all, but this party has to be cancelled."

Everyone started to boo him louder. Chanda stopped Poorna from doing the same by nudging her with her elbow.

"Please, please. Please listen to me."

The crowd generously calmed down to listen to Shantanu. Or possibly it was because the drunk, who were the majority of the crowd, got bored of booing him.

"My friends Chayansh and Chanda, who are the organizers of the party, have just got the news that their parents are coming back in an hour."

Everyone at the party started to murmur. Every single party animal teenager knew what it meant if parents showed up at a house party. It was absolute pandemonium in the house for an indefinite period. Even after that you're not relieved. Parents use such incidents as examples during arguments or to prove that you're not old enough to know what's good for you. The crowd was doing nothing else than wasting time while murmuring about the news. He knew he had to make them leave.

"Listen, listen. (The crowd stops murmuring) I know it sucks to leave such amazing party. But think of those organizers. Think of the shit-storm they'll have when their parents show up. On behalf of them, I implore you all to leave the party this instant. We're very sorry for the inconvenience."

Nobody knew what it was, his voice or his way of speech, but everyone at the party started to walk towards the door. Along with Shantanu, Chanda and Poorna looked surprised too. Chanda looked around herself and said as if he achieved an impossible task, "He did it. He's making people leave. He's shutting down the party."

XXII

It took exactly 53 minutes for *everyone* to leave, including the DJ and the bartender. The house became incredibly quiet. There were only three people left in the house, Shantanu, Chanda and Chayansh who was still passed out. Poorna had left the house on the account of meeting her boyfriend outside.

He said to Chanda, "We need to remove his shirt."

"Why?"

"So we can see the other bruised places on his body."

"Okay."

"Go get some antiseptic."

"Okay."

Chanda walked off to get the first aid box that her mother kept in the kitchen. Meanwhile, he unbuttoned Chayansh's shirt and carefully pulled the shirt off. There weren't any cuts but there were many places where his skin was reddened and there were also patches of blue among them. He may not need an antiseptic but needed an ice pack. Shantanu felt sorry. He was responsible for Chayansh's condition. He looked down on Chayansh's right hand which was hanging off the sofa, took it in his hand and whispered, "I'm sorry, bro."

After placing his hand carefully back on his chest, Shantanu got up and went up to the kitchen, knowing that Chanda would be there as well. As soon as he got there, he found her struggling for the first-aid box which was put up in one of the higher drawers. In those drawers, her mother used to put the items that were either used the least in kitchen or just needed to be stored.

Chanda had already reached her mother's height which was an exact 5'4", but those drawers were accessible only to a person with at least a height of 5'11". Shantanu was only 5'9", so he knew that he had just a fraction more chance of reaching there than her. He went behind her and, without warning, put his hands around her waist and lifted her up.

Chanda was surprised with the sudden uplift and almost lost her balance. But then she looked down and smiled at him. She never expected Shantanu to be spontaneous at such things. For all she knew, he used to suck at being spontaneous. But then again, she had recently discovered another side of him. Whatever it was, it made her happy, so she didn't want to dwell on the reason. She quickly grabbed the first-aid box and told him to lower her down. Once down, she put the box on the platform and turned towards Shantanu.

"Can I ask what are you doing?"

"Ask."

Both of them laughed at his joke.

"Okay, what are you doing?"

"I was helping you up."

"I don't recall calling for help." Chanda teased.

"But I knew you needed it."

"Can you think of something else that I would need?" Chanda got a little closer.

"Yes. Do you have any poly-bags?"

She frowned. "Yes. Why do you ask?"

"...Because we need them to make ice packs for your brother."

"Yeah, they're in the lower drawer right behind you."

Shantanu turned to look at the drawer. He walked to the drawer and bent and started to pull out some poly-bags. Once done, he got up and closed the drawer with his foot and spread the ploy-bags on the platform.

"Do you have ice?"

"...in the freezer."

"Is it enough to fill all these ploy-bags?"

"Is it necessary to fill all these bags?"

"You're right; we don't need to fill them, only the right amount."

"I'll get the ice." She started to turn towards the refrigerator. He suddenly held her hand. She stopped and turned.

"What are you doing?" Chanda said smiling. She was expecting something.

"You might want to put this first-aid box back up."

"And why would I do that?"

"Because I checked Chayansh's cuts and none of his injuries are that deep."

"Well, then why didn't you tell me before you helped me get the first-aid box?"

In response, he pulled her closer and held her waist with one hand. Their bodies were touching and both felt an increase in their heartbeats.

"I just needed a reason." He whispered softly.

Chanda already had goose bumps and felt electricity running down her spine. She was surprised at Shantanu's boldness. A month before, he couldn't even talk to her looking her in the eye. Today, he was holding her and flirting with her at kissing distance. No wonder she was too surprised to reply. But she also felt ecstatic. Like the relief someone feels drinking water after being thirsty for a long time. Like the satisfaction an artist feels after completing a masterpiece. Like the pleasure one feels after being loved by the one they loved. She slowly leaned in and kissed him. It was more of a peck, a little hurried than usual. But it was enough for Shantanu to feel it. When she stopped and looked at him, his eyes were still closed. He opened his eyes a few seconds after. Chanda looked at him and smiled. She reached back and removed his hand from her waist.

"We have my passed out brother to look after first." She said with a smile and walked to the refrigerator. He smiled and started to separate the poly-bags.

They would have kept doing their respective works if an unidentified thump wouldn't have alerted them.

XXIII

"Did you hear that?" Chanda asked while frozen in front of the refrigerator. Shantanu nodded. Another sound came. This time it wasn't a thump, but it was a tap. He knew that tap. Such sounds occurred when someone walks on a wooden floor with shoes. Another tap came; then another. Then it stopped. Because of the reverberation in an empty house, it was hard to exactly tell where the sound was coming from. But for now, the sound was coming down the hall towards their left. He started to unlace his shoes and slowly took his feet out of them.

"What are you doing?" She asked whispering.

"Whoever that is must not know where I am." He whispered back.

"Couldn't it be Chayansh? Maybe he woke up."

"He fell down approximately two flights of stairs and was heavily drunk. There is no chance of him waking up until morning."

"Wait, are you suggesting…"

"Yes, there is someone else in this house apart from us three."

"Oh my god."

"Hand me a knife, will you?"

"Shouldn't we call the police?" She said handing him the knife.

"That's a good idea but we both kept our phones in the living room, remember?"

"So, what is your plan?"

"I will follow the source of the voice and you will be heading towards the living room. I am going to check if it's really a person or something else. Once I've confirmed, I will call out to you. But in case you don't hear any sound, call the police and get out of the house as fast as you can."

"What about you and Chayansh?"

"He won't notice Chayansh for a long time. As for me, I might be able to escape or…" He let the other possibility be unspoken.

"Don't worry, it's not that dangerous. Everything will be fine." He tried to console her.

Shantanu carefully stepped out of the kitchen. Meanwhile, behind him, Chanda was getting out of her shoes as well. He turned left and started to tip-toe in that direction. He was trying to keep his breathing normal by forcing himself to breathe normally, despite his heart beating a lot faster. He didn't hear her walking towards the living room, which was good because it meant that the perpetrator didn't hear as well.

Halfway down the hallway, he heard another tap, this one being a lot smaller in magnitude. That alerted Shantanu. He stopped dead in his steps. He was sure that the perpetrator didn't change shoes, because he would've heard that. That only meant that there were two perpetrators in the house. That worsened the situation.

The already low odds of his win suddenly went down a whole notch.

Shantanu silently inhaled and started to tip-toe again. He was thinking that maybe if he used one of the perpetrators as a human shield, it might work. There were a lot of ways this could go wrong, but he wanted to believe in one of the few ways where everything worked out.

At the end of the hallway there were two ways: left and right. He listened for the tap again. No sound came. He silently went to the junction of the T-point. He carefully poked his head out and took a look in both directions. On his right, he saw someone and he quickly retracted against the wall on his right. Unfortunately, he made a sound while doing that.

For approximately 4 seconds, there was complete silence. Then he heard taps again, this time slower and getting closer after each tap. Shantanu turned the knife 180 degrees so that the tip of the knife was now downwards. He waited for the sounds to grow the right type of loud. Approximately five seconds later, the sounds of the tap came as if the perpetrator was walking right beside him.

He inhaled once and charged towards the sound. He made a quick right and jumped on the perpetrator. With him pinned down, he quickly put the knife on his throat and was about to tell him to shut up when he noticed something about the perpetrator. His face looked familiar. The realization made him a little confused.

"Alfaz?" He said with a set of confused eyebrows. Meanwhile, Alfaz looked beyond terrified. He had every reason to be. A knife was at his throat. He was trying to understand the situation when Alfaz said, "Would you mind removing the knife?"

"Oh, yes. Sorry."

Shantanu removed the knife and stood up. He looked at his right. He saw Sarthi standing right in the hallway. She looked terrified as well. But she also seemed to be frozen right in her place. Suddenly he remembered the plan. If he didn't call out to Chanda, she will call the police. It will be harder to explain the situation here, considering the mess wasn't cleaned and the house looked like a rave party scene.

"Chanda, don't call the police. It's just Alfaz and Sarthi."

"What?" Chanda's reply came a few seconds after.

It took a few seconds for Chanda to arrive at the T-point. The first question she asked was, "Where is Sarthi?" He pointed to his right and said, "She might not talk to you instantly."

"Why not?"

"I think that's because she's still in shock."

"She's in shock!? ...from what?"

"She saw me attacking Alfaz."

"Oh, god." Chanda said and walked over to Sarthi. While she was trying to recover Sarthi from the shock, Shantanu and Alfaz started to talk.

"How are you guys still here?"

"We didn't know that the party was over."

"Didn't you hear my announcement?"

"Well..."

"What?"

"When you and Chanda gave us that room, we went in there and had some more talk. Soon the talks became more personal and... intimate... so we just decided to, you know... sort of... cuddle."

"Whoa, man."

"Yeah, I know." Alfaz replied sheepishly.

"Well, what woke you guys up?"

"After we fell asleep cuddling, I woke up sometime later to pee. I noticed that there were no noises or sounds of music. I thought that the party had moved somewhere else and we were left alone in the house. That has happened to me many times, I tell you that. So I woke Sarthi up and decided to look around for a phone. That was when I heard you and I thought that there was a thief or something. And the rest is history."

XXIV

It took another 30 minutes to calm Sarthi and make both of them leave. Shantanu said while putting on his shoes, "That would be one weird story to tell."

"It sure would be."

"Hey, do you know that Alfaz and Sarthi cuddled in that room?"

"What?" She smiled mischievously, "I hope they haven't made a mess."

"You're missing the point here. My point is that Alfaz and Sarthi are very well on their way to become boyfriend-girlfriend."

"I feel happy for them."

"I am, too."

He finally tied the lace and stood near the kitchen platform and started to arrange the poly-bags. Meanwhile, Chanda just stood in her place watching Shantanu as if he was the only thing to look at in the world. It took a few seconds for him to arrange the remaining poly-bags. Then he put his hands on his hips and looked at the arrangement as if he had invented a masterpiece. He turned to find Chanda looking at him lovingly. He first smiled thinking how good it felt to be loved by someone. He could only imagine her happiness. Then he realized that they needed the ice-packs.

He snapped his fingers and Chanda blinked as if she was awoken from hypnosis. She looked at him in question.

"You were supposed to give me ice for the ice-packs."

"Yes. Sorry." She said and started to get ice from the refrigerator.

After another 20 minutes, there were multiple ice-packs on multiple spots on Chayansh's body. Once done, Shantanu stood up and looked around. The house was in a state of complete mess. There were little plastic glasses spread across the floor of the whole house at random places. Now that no one was under it, the chandelier looked ghostly and so did all the lighting. He first found the switches and turned on the original lights of the house. When Chanda looked at him in question, he replied, "I want to help you clean this house."

"No, no. it's okay. I'll do it myself."

"I know, but this was my party and so it *is* my mess."

"If you want to stay over, just say so." She said smiling.

"What?"

"Come on, I'm not as naïve as you think."

"No, seriously, I'm not asking to stay over. I just want to help you."

Chanda looked at him. She immediately saw that he was telling the truth. She sighed and stood up and said, "Okay, then. Let's get on with it."

He smiled and started to pick up the plastic cups from the floor.

XXV

"It's already half past midnight. You can stay over if you like." Chanda said for the third time since they had started cleaning. Shantanu looked at the clock. It was 12:35 A.M. She was right. He could stay over if he wanted to. He thought about staying over but then dismissed the thought. Somehow the fact that something might happen between them while Chayansh is in the house made him feel guilty again. It's amazing how guilt comes afterwards every happening like a judgmental passerby and always leaves us dreading something we shouldn't have done in the first place.

He put his hands in his pocket and said, "I really should be going. I'll apologize to Chayansh later. Please don't be mad at him, he was just drunk."

Chanda smiled at his last request. She had always liked it when Shantanu defended his friends. It gave an aura of commitment off him. She looked at his shoes and said looking up, "Okay, then. Take care."

For a few seconds both of them stood at their places. He was standing right outside the door of Chayansh and Chanda's house while she was standing holding the door open. He was looking at her face while her eyes were concentrated towards his lips. She left the door and took two steps ahead. She stood on the balls of her feet and kissed him. Apart from their lips, no other body part of theirs was touching. The kiss lasted exactly 5 seconds. He felt dazed after the kiss. Chanda felt ecstatic. She didn't know what but there was something about Shantanu's lips that she seemed to always desire. He opened his eyes three seconds after the kiss.

"What was that for?" Shantanu said smiling.

"It was a 'thank you for everything'." Chanda whispered and closed the gate.

He smiled and walked away trying to find an auto-rickshaw. It took him five minutes to find one. The proposed fare was unreasonable but he didn't want to look for another auto-rickshaw this late at night. The streets were silent like a graveyard.

Even though it has seen great development, Kota still isn't an all-night working city. Most of the pathways only had occasional vehicles either passing through or going outstation. Because of the silence, he found the sound of auto-rickshaw too loud. While sitting in the auto-rickshaw, Shantanu started to reminisce what happened between him and Chanda. The feel of the kiss sent shivers down his spine, but it also brought the guilt. It was the guilt of having romantic moments with his best-friend's sister while his best-friend was passed out in the very same house. After the guilt trip, it took some convincing and a little bribe for the guard to sneak him inside the hostel. The guard took the bribe and made a promise not to take bribe again which he knew, in the back of his mind, he would break again.

It was only when he was walking towards his room that he remembered his talk with Poorna. He remembered that she said that the solution was something she called 'love flings'. He tried to remember the definition, but he could only recall a sentence like 'momentary slips in one's mind'. He realized that the same thing happened to him. All of those were momentary slips. Assured that he was doing right, he opened the door of room no. 305 and quietly shut the door as he went inside. He turned on the lights and looked at the clock. It was 12:55 A.M. He looked around his room and took a deep breath and said, "Happy birthday, Shantanu Sharma. Well, not *my* birthday anymore."

He smiled at his own lame joke. He took off his shoes and slumped on the bed. He took off his socks on the bed and threw them towards the shoes, hoping they would land on them. He was in no mood to change clothes but he also didn't want to sleep in clothes meant only for outside. So he chose a middle option. He would rest for a minute or two and then change and sleep like a log. He wouldn't attend coaching tomorrow. He closed his eyes and stretched his arms.

The atmosphere was so silent that he could hear the clock ticking which, at other times, seemed non-existent. The monotonous ticking was lullaby to Shantanu's tired ears. His whole body relaxed and he tilted his head to his right. He would've slept in a minute if he didn't notice the sound of someone crying in his room.

The voice was of a female, which was sure. But the crying sound was so low that it gave out the feeling of the whisperings one hears in a horror movie. The scary thing was that the sound came from the direction his head was tilted towards. He was afraid to open his eyes. The crying still continued. His relaxing body went suddenly tight but remained motionless. He kept telling himself that it wasn't real— that it was some micro-sleep issue he was having— but deep down he knew that he was lying.

While Shantanu was lying there, he discovered that being motionless is in fact an art. He already had started to feel itches in different parts of his body and he was feeling the desire to turn to another position. For a few moments he tried to ignore all that. His efforts only lasted 10 seconds. After that, he mustered up all the courage he had left within himself and decided to open his left eye. He took a deep breath and opened his left eye quickly. It took some time to adjust to the bright light of the room, but once his eyes adjusted, he saw nothing. It was just his regular room wall. He opened both his eyes and looked around. He let out a sigh of relief. He was still in his room. He got up from the bed and walked in the bathroom to wash his face. He stood in front of the wash basin and turned on the faucet and splashed some water on his face.

Then suddenly he heard the same crying again. He turned off the faucet and listened hard. The sound was clearer and louder. He turned around to find the voice coming from the wall on which the shower was fitted. He thought that he should call out to identify the voice, but he thought the better of it. He had seen that same thing happening in horror movies and had always complained about the stupidity of it. The character calls out to the voice he/she is hearing and then, the ghost attacks them after noticing their presence. Then another thought struck his mind, 'what if it's the girl on the other side?'

Even though his heart was pumping faster, his brain strongly advising against the decision and his feet almost about to give up, he said, "Hello?"

His voice was so little that he scolded himself for being such a pussy. He then cleared his throat and tried to say louder, “Hello?”

The voice stopped. For a moment, he thought that he was now dead. Shivers now ran his whole body. He had stopped in whatever position he was standing. His heart had started to pump faster than ever. Drops of sweat were roaming his face and neck. Then, suddenly a voice echoed in the bathroom, loud and clear, “Yes?”

“Is it you?”

“Yes.” The reply was a few seconds late.

Shantanu felt extremely relieved. So his doubt was correct. It was the girl on the other side of the wall. Then another thought struck him, ‘*unless…*’

“How do I know that it’s you?”

“What?”

“How do I know that it’s you and not some ghost impersonating you?”

“I bloody don’t know how. You think of a way.”

At this point, he was half-convinced that it was her. But the problem was that he was only *half*-convinced.

“Tell me something that only you and I know; something that the ghost wouldn’t know.”

“You bloody daft idiot! If the ghost was haunting your bathroom, he’d already know what you and I know.”

He smiled. He was now fully convinced that it was her. Only she was able of such sarcastic, angry answers with the side of wit.

"So, you heard any crying around here?"

"I was the one crying, idiot."

"Wow, you cry too."

"Please shut up, I'm not in the mood for humor."

The answer worried Shantanu. As far as he knew, she loved humor more than anyone he knew. The fact that she was not in the mood for humor meant that something very serious had happened.

XXVI

Shantanu leaned on the wall and slid himself down. He turned his back towards the wall and sat with his legs bent and his wrists over his knees. He took 4 seconds and a deep breath before asking, "What's wrong?"

Silence.

"Hello?"

Silence.

"Are you still there?"

"Yes, I'm here."

"You didn't answer my question."

"I didn't hear your question."

"Well, I asked you what was wrong."

"From my point, everything in my life is wrong."

"Come on, it couldn't be *every*thing."

Silence.

Shantanu realized that she didn't want to answer that question. He thought of a different approach. He had read that if someone isn't relaying out what he/she is feeling, ask them a question irrelevant to their situation. In such questions, the way of answering or the words they use can give a hint to their situation. Plus they reply to your question because it doesn't relate to their current situation.

"So what are you doing right now?"

"What do you mean?" the reply came after a few long seconds.

"What are you *doing* right now? Are you sitting? Are you standing?"

"I'm sitting."

"Doing what exactly?"

"I'm mostly crying, a little drinking."

"What are you drinking?"

"It's some kind of wine. I can't spell the name. I think it's French or Italian or something."

"Wow. Imported wine. Where did you get that?"

"I'm not going to tell you that."

"Ok, then, tell me what's wrong?"

"I'm not going to tell you that either."

"Ok. Then I'll guess what happened. Tell me if I'm right. Are you ready?"

"Yes."

"I think you just got dumped."

Silence.

"Am I right?"

Silence.

"Am I right?"

Shantanu heard her crying again. He again started to worry.

"Oh, god, please. Please stop crying. Please don't cry."

"Why do you care?"

"I don't know why, I just care; okay? Now stop crying. Please." Shantanu's voice had just turned louder.

The crying voices stopped. But he could still hear her sobbing.

"I'm sorry. I shouldn't have yelled at you."

The sobbing didn't stop. He took a few deep breaths, closed his eyes and asked, "Please tell me what happened."

After a minute of silence, the reply came, "Promise me you won't tell anyone."

"Did I ever?"

XXVII

Poorna had been drinking for a while now. She was starting to feel tipsy. Yet she still had her full consciousness and wits with her. She was aware of herself sitting with her back towards the wall and holding the bottle by its neck in her right hand, taking a sip occasionally while a watch strapped to her left hand's wrist told her that it was 01:07 A.M.

She was asking herself why was she talking to this boy and why did she agree to tell him about her breakup. She didn't know, but deep down it felt kind of relieving to her talking to that boy. Once she started she couldn't stop herself. She knew that once she started talking she'd have to yield and answer him, but still she did it. So when the boy again asked for her to tell him what happened, she knew she had no choice.

"Promise me you won't tell anyone."

"Did I ever?"

She had almost said, 'no, you didn't.' but stopped herself. Instead she cleared her throat, took another sip from the bottle of wine and started.

"A few hours ago, I was at a friend's party. It was a house party. I had invited Fari— Fareed. I told you about Fareed, right?"

"Yes, you did. He's your boyfriend— *was* your boyfriend. Sorry."

"Ok, so I had invited Fareed as well. He was late, as usual. So I was waiting for him at the party. A few minutes later, I started to enjoy the party. It was a good one. I lost track of time. I kind of remained in that forgotten-time stage until I saw my friend. She was the host of the party. We hugged and chatted a little bit, but soon the party got cancelled.

"Anyways, when the party was cancelled and everyone was leaving, I got a call from Fareed. He told me to meet him in the park that was just around the corner from the house. So, I agreed to meet him there. When I reached the park, it was 10:35 P.M. These days, it gets dark pretty early, so the park was deserted. It looked like a cemetery without graves. Even though it was dark, one could still tell if someone is sitting on the benches. I walked in and saw him sitting on a bench which was shaded by a tree and behind the tree was a streetlight. The lights of the streetlight were filtering through the clump of its branches. From where I was standing, it looked like a scene from a fairy-tale. Somehow, I felt relaxed and forgot about the fact that he had called me saying that it was urgent that I meet him. I very gracefully sat beside him and hugged him.

"I had sensed that something was wrong when he didn't hug me back. But I was bedazzled enough by the location that I didn't pay it much heed. I was too stupid to recognize the tension in the air around us. When I asked him why he called me here, he didn't reply at first. It did trouble me, but I thought that maybe he scored a little low in one of his tests and maybe that's why he's upset. So I again asked him. Then he said something. He said it in such a low voice, it was almost a mumble. When I probed, he finally blurted out the most hurting words a girl in a happy relationship could hear.

'I want to break up.'

"For a moment, my mind went blank. All the fairy-tale happiness— the warm hug I just gave him, the excitement of expecting something spontaneous— just lost their charm. I was confused. Was this real? And even if it *was* real, was it some kind of sick joke? Why does he want to break up with me? What did I do? All the while I kept asking questions to myself, not uttering a single word. Possibly I failed at keeping my composure, because with one look at me, he used the 'calm down' gesture. He told me that before I freak out, I need to listen what he has to say. So I crossed my arms and looked away from him.

"He started off by saying that I was a beautiful girl and that he was happy with our relationship. Stupid excuse, I would say. If he was happy with our relationship, why would he want to break up? Anyways, so he goes on further telling me that he knows he hasn't been right to me and he thinks I deserve better than he treated these past few days. I was like, 'you think so, buddy? How touching!'

"I asked him about the reason over which he was breaking up. This was where he dropped the bomb. He told me that he was breaking up with me because all of his this month's tests have marks lower than average. I asked him what does that had to do with me. He answered that he thinks that I am the reason behind these low grades. He thinks that I am functioning in his life as a distraction. That I, and my love for him, take his mind off studies and he can't concentrate. He told me that he can't handle a relationship *and* score good marks as well. Like an arrogant postscript after an insulting letter, he also told me that I shouldn't think of this as a permanent break-up, but rather a break. He offered to love me again once he has cracked IIT."

"So what did you say?"

"What do you think I said, fool? I rejected his proposal. I told him to go stick his best grades up his ass and walked away."

"You didn't cry in front of him, right?"

"No."

"Thank god."

She started to cry again. Even though she felt a little light, she was still in grief. On the other side, Shantanu again started to worry.

"Please stop crying."

"I told you everything, damn it! Why don't you let me cry in peace?"

There was no reply from the other side. Poorna thought that he had left. For some reason, she felt even sadder. The tears started to flow again and this time, she wasn't even trying to stop them. She was convinced that she will spend the rest of her life this way: crying her guts out while she was drunk out of her mind. No heart left to spare for someone else, no mind to work out the problems of life. She took another sip of bottle and then kissed the bottle to express her gratitude for being there when needed and closed her eyes. It was then she suddenly heard a sound booming in her bathroom.

Mel roohaan de azal de roz hoye...

With the recognition of the words, she opened her eyes. For a moment, she thought she was hallucinating. The last word of the spoken sentence stretched into an *Aalaap*. Poorna realized that it was a song. But she shook her head, telling herself that it was impossible. Who would be singing a Punjabi song this late in the night? The boy on the other side was a Rajasthani and she was right now in Rajasthan. She was confirmed that it was a hallucination. She would have gone on to believe it had the song not been sung again.

Mel roohaan de azal de roz hoye…

This time she heard it loud and clear. It was too real to be hallucination. But it wasn't possible; she knew it. How could it have been possible that someone was singing a Punjabi song? She put the bottle down and quickly shouted, "Hello? Who's this?"

"It's me." The reply was quick.

"Who?" She was a bit confused; maybe because she was tipsy.

"It's me; the boy from the other side."

"What? How are you singing a Punjabi song?"

"I learned it."

"When did you learn it?"

"I do have a life outside of the shower."

"How do you know this song?"

"It's Ghulam Ali's 'Heer'. Why? Do you know this song?"

Poorna took some time to reply. It had been forever since she had talked about her father to anybody. It wasn't an issue of being hurt by old memories; she felt that talking about her father only earned her sympathy in other people's eyes. 'Sympathy is just a taunt wrapped in grief.' It was a theory that she believed in.

"My… my father used to sing it to me."

"…Used to?"

"Yes. Um, he's no more."

"I bet you miss him."

"Yes."

"My parents are dead, too."

"…Both of them?"

"Yes."

"Well, I guess we're not so different after all."

"I don't think that we were ever that different."

Poorna didn't reply for a few seconds. She was now feeling guilty for judging him.

"Why are you doing this?" Her voice had become hoarse.

"What?"

"You are singing to a drunken, heart-broken girl who you don't know in the middle of the night while sitting in your bathroom."

"You think that I have an ulterior motive behind this, an agenda."

She didn't reply to that. Shantanu continued.

"Well, it might come to you as a surprise that I don't have any agenda behind this. I have no hope of getting anything in return."

"Then why would you be doing this at all?"

"Let's just say that it's because I care for you."

Poorna felt somewhat happy on hearing this. But the feeling was quickly replaced with alarm. She knew how much it hurt when ties broke. And her tie with this boy was getting stronger by the minute. It wasn't just harmful for her, but also for him.

"Please don't care so much for me."

"Why?"

"Because I'm not worth it."

"I believe that's up to me to decide."

Even with the tears resting on her cheeks, a smile crept up on Poorna's face.

"So you'll sing for me?"

"Yes."

"And when the song ends, what then?"

"I'll sing it again from the start."

"How long will you sing like this?"

"...As long as it takes."

The smile was back on her face fully. She felt happy and somewhat grateful to him. She didn't realize that time but he had been the only person to make her smile with tears in her eyes since her father's death. Last time she smiled like that was when her father was on his deathbed. In his last moments, he cracked a joke about marriage and the 13 year-old Poorna, cradled right beside him in his hug, laughed out loud.

On the other side, Shantanu started to sing on receiving no reply from the girl.

Mel roohaan de azal de roz hoye,

Te sacchey ishq di new tamer hoyi.

Phull khir gaye paak mohabbataan de,

Koyi ranjha hoya koi heer hoyi...

Poorna closed her eyes and let some tears escape. She was taking in the melody of it. She never felt the peace like she felt now. As long as that song and its reverberations were around her, nothing could be wrong with the world.

She didn't know if it was the song or the wine finally kicking in, but she felt physically light. After what seemed like a very long time in her life, she felt the true happiness. Like the happiness a child gets on seeing his/her mother come back home even if that's the regular drill for both of them. Like the happiness someone gets when visiting a new place and finding it more beautiful than expected. Like the happiness one gets when he/she finds love. Meanwhile, the song continued.

vela aa tukeya azmaishaan da,

baneya but to rooh dilgeer hoyi.

Dukh dard vichh de umraan de,

Te aashqaan saadkaan di taqdeer hoyi.

As he continued to sing, Poorna opened her eyes slightly and picked up the bottle. After looking at it for a while, she put the bottle as far away as her hand would allow and closed her eyes. She didn't any other intoxication, his voice was alcoholic enough.

XXVIII

...K*oi ranjha hoya koi heer hoyi...*

Poorna woke up to the continued song. She found a momentary figure of her father smiling down on her. This jerk-woke her up. But he was gone when she woke up. Meanwhile, the song was still going on, surprisingly, with the same rhythm as last night.

vela aa tukeya azmaishaan da,

baneya but to rooh dilgeer hoyi.

Dukh dard vichh de umraan de,

Te aashqaan saadkaan di taqdeer hoyi.

"Hey." She called out. The song stopped. The first reply that came was, "Are you feeling better now?"

The reply brought a smile to her face and made her feel sad about sleeping. She nodded while replying, as if he could see her.

"Yes, I'm feeling much better now."

"Are you feeling hung-over?"

"Yes, but only a little bit."

"Well, I suggest then you get yourself better in about... one hour."

"What's after one hour?"

"In an hour, we're going to celebrate."

"Why?"

"Because it's your first morning as a single; and that's worth celebrating."

"I…" Poorna started but Shantanu cut her off.

"No. I don't want to hear about this. I'll be waiting for you after an hour."

"But, listen…" she started but stopped when she heard the sound of the door closing.

She sighed and went in her room. It had been a long time since she had felt hung-over. But she knew that she'll easily survive, given her history with drinking and hang-overs.

Surprisingly, she remembered everything that happened last night to the minutest detail. Although, she couldn't decide what should she do. With every memory of last night, the realization that she and Fareed broke up also hit her. With the realization came the feeling of detachment and loneliness. Even though the boy on the other side was making efforts for her, she appreciated them but couldn't accept them. The fact that he had no agenda behind this troubled Poorna's mind further.

She brushed and drank lots of water in hope of curing her headache. She suddenly remembered that pills she had kept especially if she ever started to drink again. She found her first-aid box and looked in it. She found the pills and were about to take one when the urge to check for expiration date stopped her. She checked the date and found that it expired 2 months ago. She threw the pills in the dustbin and picked up her towel and spare undergarments from the closet. Before going inside the bathroom, she turned to look around the room, thinking that maybe she should go out and take a walk in the nearby park. But some thought at the back of her mind pushed her into the shower.

After 56 minutes, Shantanu was back in the bathroom and was putting the soap on the floor and his phone on the soap holder. He waited for a sound from the other side. He had planned about this; but now that he had to execute this plan, he was nervous. People are hopeful only when they make any plan for the first time.

But he felt his nervousness project itself when he heard the sound of the door from the other side.

He shook his head slightly, inhaled and exhaled deeply a few times and straightened his back, as if ready to receive a formal salute. After five seconds, he said, "Are you feeling better now?"

"A little bit, I think."

"Okay, then." He said and inhaled deeply and then announced, "So, ladies and gentlemen, we have big news for today. Our revered guest has officially resigned from the love firm and decided to join our brethren of singlehood."

He knew how ridiculous he sounded, but that's what he wanted. He wanted to sound ridiculous and unreasonable. Because what he was doing was unreasonable. He wanted to make her laugh and the best way, as he felt, would be to portray himself as a joker. He didn't know where to place this desire to placate and please someone you don't even know. Was it compassion? Was it guilt? He didn't know. Not once did the word *love* cross his mind. Ironic.

When the announcement was finished, he heard a chuckle from the other side. He knew he wasn't imagining it. He smiled fully with unknown hope. He continued.

"On this special occasion, I, the fabulous RJ, the marvelous singer and a witty son-of-a-bitch, would like to dedicate a sing to her singlehood. And don't worry, ma'am, the song is on the house."

Shantanu turned to his mobile phone and touched the play button. An EDM-type tune started to play. The tune repeated itself three times and then he started to sing.

Dono ke dono single,

Dono ke dono pagal,

Dono ke dono single,

Dono ke dono pagal,

Dono ke dono single,

Dono ke dono pagal,

Dono ke dono single,

Dono ke dono pagal,

Pa-pa-pa-pagal-pagal.

It was then the iconic tune of the song started to play. The tune itself seemed to dance and was making them move their feet as well. On the other side, all the worries of Poorna had suddenly vanished with the onset of the song. She was enjoying every bit of it. She felt as if she's on some kind of beach party. The shower drops seemed to be jumping with a different sense of cheerfulness. She danced as long as the tune continued, and then the voice from the other side boomed in the bathroom.

Let me-let me-let me,

Let me tell you something,

We live only once,

Main tainu right treat karaan,

Baby, give me one chance.

O, chadd relationship ka panga,

Saala, breakup ka stress,

Just be single and we mingle,

It's feeling the best.

Now throw your hands up in the air,

And hold them up high,

'cause we go party all night,

I'm single I ain't shy… shy.

Dono ke dono single,

Dono ke dono pagal,

Ye ishq bewakoofi,

Aa milke kare chal,

Jeena hai toh jeena hai,

Toh kyun soche kya hoga kal.

Dono ke dono single,

Dono ke dono pagal,

Ye ishq bewakoofi,

Aa milke kare chal,

Jeena hai toh jeena hai,

Toh kyun soche kya hoga kal.

Dono ke dono single…

The tune had changed to a more EDM-type version of the previous one.

Meanwhile, both of them danced under their showers like they would at a beach party. Poorna had forgotten about her breakup already. As soon as she heard the song, she felt the freedom of being single. As the song suggested, she felt single and crazy at the same time. She also chimed in.

Hoon chaubis ka main,

Hai baees ki tu,

Akela main,

Akeli hai tu bhi,

Handsome sa hoon main,

Hai cute si tu,

Mila le dil, mila le bakhoobi.

Jo tu rubaru hai,

Toh pyaar shuru hai, shuruhai,

Na tu sharam kar,

Thoda reham kar,

Aa pyaar kar, chal,

Dono ke dono single,

Dono ke dono pagal,

Ye ishq bewakoofi,

Aa milke kare chal,

Jeena hai toh jeena hai,

Toh kyun soche kya hoga kal.

Dono ke dono single…

With the onset of another EDM tune, both of them had exhausted themselves by dancing. As he danced, he suddenly felt something with the change in tune. He stopped dancing.

What he was feeling *was* the sense of the upcoming stanza of the song, but along with that, Shantanu felt something else. He felt inside him a plea, an urge to confess. He thought of conveying it through the song. The situation seemed fit. If she didn't understand, then no harm done, but if she did, then...

With such thoughts accumulating in his mind, he smiled and started to sing the next lyrics as best as he could, hoping that she might understand, hoping that she might reciprocate.

Main uljha hoon,

Tu suljha de;

Main jaan doonga,

Tu dil toh de;

Tu zid dil ki,

Tu hadh meri,

Tu lat meri.

As soon as he started to sing this stanza, Poorna felt the rhythm change. Not the rhythm of the song, but the rhythm of her heart. She felt her heart accelerate, but it wasn't because of dancing. She had stopped dancing at the end of the second stanza. She could feel something in the air around her, but it wasn't humidity. It felt some kind of aura-like substance that seemed to emanate from the wall, or rather, from behind the wall. She felt tension, but she couldn't believe herself. It was romantic tension. *Is he singing it for me? Is he trying to propose me through a song?* She questioned herself. But before she could reach to any conclusions, the stanza had reached its final lines. Her 'singing reflex' told her to be ready. So, she brushed aside the thoughts, tried to ignore the tension and started to sing.

Kehne ko khushi hai,

Par sach mein khudkhushi hai,

Khudkhushi hai,

Yaara zara sambhal,

Yoon na jao fisal,

Chadd pyaar ko, chal,

Dono ke dono single,

Dono ke dono pagal,

Ye ishq bewakoofi,

Aa milke kare chal,

Jeena hai toh jeena hai,

Toh kyun soche kya hoga kal.

Dono ke dono single,

Dono ke dono pagal,

Ye ishq bewakoofi,

Aa milke kare chal,

Jeena hai toh jeena hai,

Toh kyun soche kya hoga kal.

Dono ke dono single…

With the end of the song, both of them felt tired, but also relieved. He felt he was in the terribly confused place of one sided-love. Both of them didn't say anything to each other until they wiped themselves. Poorna was thinking about the 'supposed' proposal. She thought of the incident and she knew it wasn't a figment of her imagination. But instead of feeling angry or sad towards the boy, she felt shy and happy. She thought of the way as cute and she had never felt such intensity of love in a person.

Maybe it was the 'aura' of his love or maybe because she had just broken up or maybe it was her own feelings, but she felt crazily happy. She felt the need to say something, but she felt nervous. What if it was her own feeling that she sensed? This question formed circular barriers in her mind, her rejection bias stopping her from confessing. She had started to feel something for the boy. The feeling felt like it was there all the time, but was clouded by her relationship. She wanted to confess so bad, but the fear of rejection was gripping her throat, making those three words harder to escape her mouth. So, she chose a middle route. If he didn't understand, no harm done, but if he did, then...

Before leaving the bathroom, she said a few words that meant something else but felt exactly like how she felt.

"I like your voice."

On the other side, Shantanu smiled as if he understood.

XXIX

"You're late." Chanda said six days after Shantanu and Poorna's bathroom confession.

Shantanu was panting from the running he was doing. It was noon of the winter, when the sun is at its best. People had come into the park to have a slice of heaven-like warmth. Children were playing cricket regardless of the population around them. Couples were sitting either on the benches or on the grass or walking hand-in-hand throughout the park. Married couples were sitting on the grass having animated conversations and the old folks were either having discussions sitting in circles at various places in the park or praying in the nearby temple.

He bent down and put his hands on his knees. His shirt had changed color due to the sweat and his knees felt like they would fold any second against his will. He took a few deep breaths and looked up at Chanda. She was wearing a red and black checkered shirt with its sleeves folded up till her forearms, exposing mostly her wrists, along with dark blue jeans and black bellies. Her denim jacket was lying beside her in a crumpled state. She was wearing her hair open which were curling at the ends. With her perfectly oval face and a slight proud-angry expression on her face, she looked like a beautiful temptress. It was hard not to stare at her. Shantanu was doing that too. She decided to gain his attention even though she liked when he stared at her. She cleared her throat. He looked at her face.

"What?"

"You're beautiful." He replied without thinking.

A smile came on Chanda's face. "You're forgiven."

She patted the bench with her right hand. Shantanu, thankful for the seat, literally slumped on the bench. While he was having deep breaths to bring his body from hectic to normal state, Chanda watched him and smiled as if he was a child having fun.

Two minutes later, the sweat on his forehead had disappeared, even though the traces of sweat remained on his shirt. But during those two minutes, Shantanu was trying to grasp the reason Chanda called him here. He was a bit surprised when she called him to meet up. When he asked her the location, she told him to come to the park near their house. He was a bit taken aback. Why would she want to meet him at a park which was near *their* house? Something was off, and he wanted to find out, so he said okay. She had given him the time of 12:30 P.M. It was the time her tuitions started.

He finally opened his eyes and turned to his left to face Chanda. She looked around and he looked at her in confusion. What was wrong? Was someone following her? Is someone stalking her? Is someone threatening her? While he was engrossed in these thoughts, Chanda suddenly cupped his face and kissed him.

Chanda was looking at their potential watchers. The bench they were sitting on was obscured from the view by the trees and bushes growing behind it. The children in front of them were too busy playing cricket. Nobody was walking rounds around the park, and the old folks were too busy bickering about the world. It was the perfect opportunity. Chanda felt enormously attracted towards Shantanu's lips, and she thought it was a good opportunity. So she cupped his face and gave him a small kiss. The kiss lasted 2 seconds. It was rushed but it was exciting. She quickly regained her composure and sat as if nothing had happened while Shantanu was trying to come back from that feeling, his eyes closed. He took two whole seconds to recover. She looked at the show and smiled. She was starting to like the effect she, or rather her lips, had on him.

When he finally came back to reality, he found Chanda looking at the park as if nothing had happened. But he knew it wasn't his imagination. Her lopsided and rather excited smile was enough proof.

"What was that for?" Shantanu asked playfully.

"It was a 'thanks for coming'."

"So what happened? Why did you call me here?"

Chanda opened her mouth to say something, but then stopped. She looked at the park for a while. He was patiently waiting for an answer. She took a deep breath and turned towards him.

"Look, what I'm about to say to you is going to sound super-forward. So, try to be normal about it. It's not a spur-of-the-moment decision. I've given it thought and time equally."

"You're not going to ask me to marry you, right?" Shantanu joked.

Chanda chuckled. The honest-yet-humorous attitude of him worked almost everywhere.

"No, I wasn't going to. But there is something that I want to ask you."

"Okay."

"What do you think about relationship?"

"…the term 'relationship'?"

"No. Let me rephrase that. What do you think about *being* in a relationship?"

I think I know where this is heading. "Well, if you ask me, relationships are commitments towards a person. Relationship is not something that just grows out of the blue like a wild plant. It has to be nurtured, coaxed and cared for. It takes time and an investment of your-self. So, being in a relationship is only successful when you are ready for a commitment."

"So, are you?"

"Am I what?"

"Are you ready?"

"…For what?"

"Are you ready for a commitment?"

It's just what I feared. "Are you proposing me?"

Chanda's cheeks went red. She smiled coyly and looked away. That was proof enough for him. His mind started to process information faster than his brain could handle. He was trying to find a way out.

God, isn't there any other way?

XXX

Shantanu was in dilemma. He knew he didn't love Chanda, but he didn't want to break her heart as well. He knew that she will resent him. And that was exactly what he didn't want. Chayansh and Chanda were two of his best friends whom he loved equally. Chanda's efforts had broken down his wall and had complicated their friendship.

"Yes." She answered looking into his eyes hopefully.

"Listen, Chanda, I…" Shantanu stammered.

Chanda's expressions changed to worry.

He took a deep breath and replied, "I'm going to have to say no."

She blinked as if she couldn't believe it was real.

"What?" It was all that she could say.

"Calm down, Chanda. Listen to me first. I can explain everything."

"Okay, then. Explain everything." She said curtly.

He opened his mouth and then closed it. How could he explain what happened between them? It wasn't an act of friendship. It wasn't lust. How could he classify that in any category other than love? But Shantanu knew that he didn't love Chanda. So why did he lead her on? Was it attraction he felt towards Chanda? He figured that maybe this was the reason. Maybe she will understand. But 'maybe' wasn't an option.

"Okay, I can't explain it." He bowed his head.

"What?"

"What?"

"What can't you explain?"

"Um... I can't explain why we tried to kiss that night outside village 69. I can't explain why we kissed at my birthday party. I can't explain why I led you on afterwards. I can't explain why I showed you the love that wasn't there in the first place."

For a few moments, both Chanda and Shantanu remained silent. Both of them were in deep thought.

"So you don't love me?" Chanda broke the silence. Her voice was hoarse.

He felt a knot tightening in his chest. He bowed his head and shook his head in 'no'.

"So why... why didn't you say it to me that time? Why did you make me go through this?" She held her head in her hands. She looked and sounded depressed.

Shantanu sighed and said while shaking his head, "Because I was selfish, Chanda. I wanted to feel that love you felt towards me. I felt attracted to you. I wanted to know how it feels to be loved. I was selfish, Chanda. I'm sorry." His voice was overwhelmed with guilt.

Silence crept again in between. Whilst sitting on two corners of the same bench, both of them looked like a couple who had a fight recently. Shantanu was feeling guiltier like never before. In the long list of his mistakes, he would rank this as his number 1 mistake. The silence was excruciating. It made him worry. He wanted Chanda to lash out, to cry and scream at him, create a scene, anything that would show that she still cared about him. He wanted her to believe in the idea of love, because that was a part of her he admired. Because of her, he saw the physical manifestation of love. It was something he had forgotten long ago.

Even though tears were threatening to flow out any second, he stopped them with all his emotional blockades he had remaining. He said, trying to control the hoarseness in his voice, "I know that whatever I did isn't justifiable. It doesn't matter if I had a reason. I still did you wrong."

When he saw that there was no reaction from Chanda, he added, "I would heartily accept any punishment you would give me, just please don't be like that. Please be my friend again. I can't see you like this."

"Fine." Suddenly Chanda's voice struck his ears. He turned his head as if in shock.

"I'm sorry. What?"

"I said, 'fine'."

He smiled, relieved.

"So here is my punishment."

His smile disappeared.

"You have to complete my two wishes."

"What wishes?"

"Any two wishes that I want at any given point of my life."

Shantanu processed each word of that sentence and said, "Okay."

"Ok. So my first wish is that you tell Chayansh everything."

What? What did she say? "What?" Shantanu blinked twice before saying.

"Yeah. I want *you* to tell Chayansh about everything that happened between you and me, no detail left out."

"I can't do that."

"You just said you will accept any punishment I give you."

"I..." Shantanu started to stammer.

"Well, this is my punishment for you. Just in case you need time to build up the courage, I'm giving you till Sunday. After Sunday, I will tell everything to Chayansh myself and to my mom and dad as well." Although she had tried to sound threatening, Shantanu realized the fragility in her voice. She said it like she was being told to say it even though she didn't want to.

Every human has the gift of self-destruction. Humans can choose on how to lead their lives. Chanda had decided to gradually self-destruct.

XXXI

"Would you like to have some *paani patashas*?" Shantanu offered after a minute of silence. Chanda had already announced her verdict and was already mad at him, but not more than she was at herself. She looked at him with disbelief.

How could he be so casual at such a big topic? Chanda thought.

She was about to decline his offer rudely when Shantanu said, "Listen, I know what you must be thinking. 'How can I be so casually asking you this when something such devastating has happened?' But friends should be friends in all conditions. Old relations never fade with the onset of a new one. 'Would we become lovers?' is a question to answer later. What we have right now is each other's friendship. And I don't want to lose that. So this is just me, asking as a friend. Would you like to have some *paani patashas*?"

Chanda didn't reply. She joined her hands and put them on her mouth. Shantanu was half-convinced that she would decline. He knew that he should take her silence as rejection and walk away from here. But the only problem was that he was only *half*-convinced. So he stayed where he was. After 3 minutes of patient waiting, she got up and started to walk away. He bowed his head in disappointment. He was starting to think that he should have chosen his words more carefully. He thought that maybe he wasn't convincing enough. He was cursing himself for making such stupid slips of mind. It had not only complicated everything but also jeopardized his friendship with both Chayansh and Chanda.

"Hey." A voice sounded in his ears. He looked up to see who it was. He saw Chanda standing at one of the gates of the park and calling out to him. He stood up, his mind taking numerous dips in the ocean of confusion. She gestured him to come. He walked over to her with a frown on his face. Why was she behaving like this? She looked happy. A moment earlier she looked like a depressed middle-aged woman and now she was an extroverted, fun-loving teenager.

While Shantanu was engrossed in these thoughts, he didn't realize that he had walked up to her and stopped. He was looking like an autistic child standing with his head bowed a little and a frown on his face along with the dilemma-look. He was jerked to reality when Chanda grabbed his collar and said, "Let's have a *paani patasha* face-off. The loser buys all the eaten and the will-be-eaten *patashas*."

For a moment, he couldn't believe that this was the girl he had just refused to love.

"'Life is like a tree in autumn. Either you eat the leaves before they fall or you let them fall before you can eat them.'"

"What?"

"Don't you remember, stupid? It's one of your late-night epiphanies."

"Maybe I slept like a log after this one, because I don't remember it."

"Well, I do. I and Chayansh write down these words of wisdom as they come."

"Okay, that's just exaggeration."

"Come on, now. Those *paani patashas* aren't going to finish themselves up." Chanda said and walked out of the gate.

He walked out the gate and followed behind her. He was smiling as they both walked, one after the other.

It was obvious that she won the face-off. Not because Shantanu let her win, but because he already had his lunch before meeting Chanda. She was walking slowly and alongside he was walking slowly as well. They both were too full to walk normally. She was regretting the number of extra *patashas* she ate after winning. She was very well full when she won, but just to spite Shantanu, she ate 20 *patashas* extra. She could actually feel her stomach stretching itself. She found even breathing difficult. The distance between her house and the *paani patasha* stall wasn't much, but traversing that distance was becoming difficult with each passing second, plus she felt like she would puke any second.

Shantanu looked at his watch. It was 01:27 P.M. He couldn't believe that everything happened in just one hour. But he was relieved. He was relieved because even though he rejected her she still enjoyed with him like his friend. He looked at her from the corner of his eyes. She was holding her denim jacket on her forearm like a waiter. She walked with small, careful steps and her belly was bulged out and seemed to bounce with her walking. She was looking up occasionally with a pained look on her face.

"We should go back to the park and sit there a while." Shantanu said.

Chanda looked at him and asked, "What's the time?"

He looked at his watch and said, "It's almost half past one."

She said, "Then we can't sit in the park. I have to go."

"Where are you going?"

"Home. The duration of my tuition is over."

"So where's your bag?"

"I left it on the front door of my house."

"Aren't you worried your parents might see it?"

"No. I put it in the middle of my mom's garden."

"Oh, ok then." He said. He knew which place she was talking about.

Ever since they were born, Chanda and Chayansh shared everything, from rooms to toys and even books. But the same case wasn't with their parents. Both of them believed in having private spaces; which is why there were some things which they both had labeled as their private.

The corner room on the second floor was Chandrashekhar's private study. The almirah in the first floor bedroom was Chaaya's private wardrobe. Similarly, the outside garden with the grass and shrubs belonged to Chandrashekhar and was managed and cared for by him and the potted plants on the front door and the creepers on the terrace were Chaaya's responsibility, known between the twins and Shantanu as 'dad's garden' and 'mom's garden' respectively.

She proceeded to mom's garden and he followed her. She opened the metal gate slowly and without any sound and Shantanu followed suit. The stone-clad pathway had its borders lined with flower pots and beyond those flower pots, were two big patches of grass on either side of the pathway. There were different types of flowers and trees growing in between the grass, ranging from mango tree to pink roses. Even with the polluted environment of Kota, the plants in the flower pots and the trees in the grass flourished. At the end of the pathway, three marble steps showed the way to the porch which circled the entire house. On the end of that porch, was the door through which one entered the house. Around the door, the 'mom's garden' thrived, many pots with small plants ranging from bougainvillea to a few bonsai plants. The pots were arranged carelessly around both sides of the door and formed a sort of inward arc. Chanda walked to her right side and leaned forward. It was almost magical. The bag's size made it hide perfectly between the pots. When she took out the shoulder-length bag, it was almost as if she produced it from Doraemon's pocket. She strapped on the bag, turned towards him and shrugged a little like an advertisement model.

The silence had crept again in between them. Both of them didn't know what to say. The intricacies of conversations are always very fragile. Conversations become difficult just because people *feel* they can't go further.

"So, I'll see you on Sunday, then?" She tried to sound normal and failed.

"Ok, then, bye."

"Bye."

Both of them said their byes, but none of them had the courage to walk away. The hope of her forgiveness made Shantanu hold his ground while the wish for traces of love in his eyes froze Chanda to the spot. They stood at the front door, facing each other, gazing into each other's eyes for a full minute. She traversed the gap between them in two steps and looked in his eyes directly. For a few seconds, they both looked like a movie poster, with him looking slightly down to her and her looking upwards at him, both of them close to each other physically. She slowly cupped his face and stood on the balls of her feet and kissed him. He, without any reason, reciprocated. He put his hands on her waist and pulled her closer. The kiss was neither loving nor rushed nor thirsty. It had a certain tinge of sadness to it. Other than that, He could feel the desperation of one last try in it.

After complete 15 seconds, they both parted. Both of them felt strangely relieved. It was as if they had exchanged their thoughts through that kiss. Like a big load was off their heads.

"See you on Sunday." She said and started to walk towards the door.

"What was that for?" He tried to stop her.

"It was a 'farewell of love', Shantu." Her voice was hoarse.

She turned and rung the doorbell. Getting the hint, he walked away. She turned to watch him walk away. He didn't even look back once. She walked in the house and went up to her room.

Inside the attached bathroom, while washing her face, she could feel the hot tears streaming out of her eyes. She washed her face again and again, the ferocity increasing with each splash. Finally she broke down and sat on the floor of the bathroom, crying her tears. She now knew how love bids farewell.

XXXII

When Shantanu walked away from Chanda, he had every intention of turning back to look at her just one more time. To see the love she felt for him, to feel it. But he knew it was not to be. He and Chanda were not on the same page about love. But he knew that he was the reason that they were not on the same page. The weight of the *paani patashas* still hung on his body like a camel's hump, but it was less troubling now.

The last time Shantanu felt such level of confusion was when he was deciding whether or not to come to Kota. He knew the amount of stress and anxiety he suffered in that time. He was in dilemma. If he chooses to tell Chayansh everything, he might lose both of his best friends; but if he chooses not to tell everything, he will *surely* lose both of his best friends as well as any chance of getting them back. Even though both options were different, one thing was common in both the options; all three of them would go through a hell lot of suffering, him, Chayansh and Chanda.

While he was thinking all this, he didn't know where he was heading, at least consciously. His feet moved like they were programmed mechanical appendages. It's amazing how we have this system of self-tracking. No matter where we are, we somehow always end up where we want to be. Just like that, he had reached his hostel without even knowing it. He looked around. It was still afternoon. He looked at his watch. It was 01:47 P.M. He couldn't believe that it had been just 20 minutes. He felt like the whole day must've been gone by now. He was expecting to see evening around him. For a few seconds, he stood and looked at the hostel as if he had been seeing it for the first time.

"Yes, what do you want?"

He looked down to see who it was. What he saw made him clench his jaw. Standing in front of him was Aaradhna Makhija, the hostel warden of A & A boys' hostel. She was wearing a night gown with flowery prints on it along with an extra-long maroon petticoat which peeked out of the night gown a little to touch the ground. She was wearing slippers that were too big for her feet and extended beyond her heel like she had wore flippers the wrong way. Her hairs were a mess which was weakly held together by a hair-band.

The changes after the 'incident' in both the sisters were remarkable. Shantanu had heard about the hostel from his next door neighbor, Mahesh.

Both the sisters were only 21 when they started the hostel. At the age of 25, they both had broken up after the mishaps. It had been three years since then. So, they both were barely over 28. But with their pregnant-looking bellies, overly visible double chins and wobbling arms and thighs, they looked like they had crossed the age of 45. This type of body not only gained them sympathy but also a reputation. Everyone in the neighborhood knew better than to try to communicate with either of the sisters. It was the latest tattle that both the sisters have gone slightly mad and they also have rapid mood swings to the point which indicates that both of them might be possessed, possibly by the same ghost. The possession part was obviously false, but the neighbors were right about the sisters getting slightly mad. As soon as he saw her, he straightened his back as if he was a soldier reporting to his senior. Meanwhile, Aaradhna was getting impatient.

"Tell me, boy, what do you want?"

"I just want to get into the hostel."

"Why? Do you have someone here who is related to you somehow?"

"No, ma'am. I live here."

"As what? As a guard?"

"No, warden ma'am; as a student."

"In that case, I'm going to need your room number, your name and identity proof along with the ID card of the coaching you go to."

"Ma'am, there's no need for that. I'm telling the truth. I live here."

Shantanu's eyes wandered around and found the guard coming out of the toilet which was behind the guard's cubicle. He suddenly felt a surge of relief. He excitedly pointed towards the guard and said, "He knows me. Ask *him* if I live here."

Aaradhna turned to look at the guard. The guard froze in his position by seeing the warden out of her quarters. He got a feeling that he might be in trouble because of the kid standing in front of the warden. Did he tell on him? But that would kick both of them out of the hostel. Was he trying to bring that same girl back in the hostel? He was mentally rebuking himself to take bribes. Meanwhile,

Aaradhna became impatient again. She waved her hand to call the guard. The guard walked over to them thinking all the wrongs he had done in his job of guard. When he stood face-to-face, he straightened his back and did an almost formal salute to which she didn't respond.

"Why were you not here?" She said so curtly that it felt like an accusation.

"I was in the toilet, ma'am." The guard's voice felt shaking.

"What were you doing in the toilet?"

"What everyone does, ma'am." The guard said after a few seconds of silence.

"I know what people like you go to toilets for. Anyways, do you know this kid?" She pointed towards Shantanu.

"Yes, ma'am." The guard replied almost instantly.

Aaradhna looked at the kid for a few seconds and then turned to the guard and said, "I noticed that you're going to toilets too much these days. Your job is to guard, not to visit the toilet. Understood?"

"Yes, ma'am."

As soon as Aaradhna walked away, both of them heaved a sigh of relief.

"Thank you." He said to the guard.

"Don't get in front of her again. I might not be around every time to save you."

"Yes. I'll be wary about that."

Both of them shook hands and he went up to his room while the guard sat back in his cubicle.

When Shantanu entered the room, he looked at the watch again. It was 2:02 P.M. He hoped that at least it would've been an hour. He slumped on the bed looking at the ceiling. His hands were lying on his sides like he was trying to make snow angels while his feet were dangling off the bed with the shoes still in them.

It was only after two seconds that he smelled something. A foul smell. He knew that kind of smell. It was the smell of sweaty underarms. He turned his head both sides and smelled both of his underarms, and both of them smelled badly. He thought that he should shower. Even though the concept of showering in the middle of the day was unappealing to him, the smell of his sweaty underarms was far more unappealing. He took off his shoes, threw his socks on the bed and pulled out his towel from the closet. He walked to the bathroom and turned on the switch of the geyser. With his towel hanging on his shoulder, he took out his extra undergarments and took all of his clothes off except for undergarments.

After waiting for two minutes, he walked in the bathroom. He hung his towel along with his undergarments on a metal bar near the shower on his right side. He turned on the shower and the warm and immensely soothing shower drops started to fall on him. Just when he had started to enjoy the shower, he was startled by a loud noise.

"WHAT THE FUCK!"

XXXIII

It had been another day of bunk for Poorna, but she hadn't decided that voluntarily. For some reason, her alarm didn't go off today, so she didn't wake at the right time. When she woke up, her phone showed that it was 11:00 A.M. After waking up, she spent the next 15 minutes trying to figure out a way of getting the notes of the classes she missed today, because she sure as hell wasn't going to enter the class in the middle. After negotiating the price of her friend's notes for a *paani-patasha* feast, she looked around in confusion as to what to do now. She thought that she should get ready. So she got up to brush her teeth, but stopped midway because she thought she should check her phone first.

She unlocked the phone. There were no missed calls or messages. She turned on the internet and whatsapp and Facebook messages started to flood in. She firstly went on whatsapp and checked all the messages. All of those were from groups she was a member of, like her group of classmates named 'Successors' and her family whatsapp group 'Sher Singhs' and a few others from her school days.

She turned to Facebook and checked. There were multiple pending friend requests, some tag notifications and some school friends of hers had sent messages asking when they could have a reunion. She locked her phone and stared blankly at the ceiling. She was expecting something from

Fareed. Even a simple 'hi' would've satisfied her. She went over and checked Fareed's profile, but she couldn't find it. She figured that he must've deleted his profile. She felt sad. Even though he made it clear that he wouldn't be in touch in whatsoever form, she still wanted him to be in touch with her. Human minds are fragile. They always seek out emotions that aren't there in the first place, just because they want to feel something. Because if we don't feel, what better work are we left with?

She started to reluctantly surf through Facebook. She accepted some more friend requests of the people she knew and just threw away the phone on the bed. She slumped on the bed with moist eyes. It was only after a minute that tears started to flow down her eyes. For a few seconds, she cried silently, staring blankly at the ceiling while her eyes were overflowing with tears. She then turned around and buried her head in the pillow and screamed. She screamed like she never had before. The scream had the feeling of plead and loss in it. It was the scream of a child after losing a beloved pet.

Like any tantrum, this one faded fast as well; she had started to sob now. The sobbing lasted three minutes and she pulled out her head from the pillow. It was completely drenched in the places where she had wiped her tears and her nose. It was a disgusting sight. It looked like a rudimentary butterfly made from tears and mucus.

It was a weird feeling. Even after crying her eyes out, she didn't feel relieved. It was like the crying hadn't reduced whatever weight was on her head. She felt heavier. With the unknown, invisible weight on her head, she brushed and slumped on the bed again. She thought of ordering a pizza and staying in her room all day watching videos on

YouTube until her eyes started to ache. But then she put a stop to the thought-train and decided that she should shower first. She went to the bathroom and turned on the geyser. In this winter, she knew it would be about 9 minutes for the water to be warm at the right temperature. So she turned on her phone and started to watch videos on YouTube. After three or four videos, she threw the phone back on the bed and started to get undressed and pulled out her undergarments and her two towels. She went in the bathroom and put her two towels on the metal bar on her right side along with the undergarments.

She stood in a position where the shower drops would only reach her chest and she would have to lean in to bring her head under the shower. She put her hand on the knob and twisted it with a jerk so that the knob would be turned on to the full. She didn't want any drop to be wasted.

As soon as the shower drops hit her body, she shrieked out, "WHAT THE FUCK!" and jumped away from the stream of the shower. She had expected a warm and soothing shower. And what she felt right now was the stream of water so hot it felt like it came from hell itself.

XXXIV

As soon as he heard those words, he was immediately alerted. He put his head out of the stream of the shower and asked, "Is that you?"

On the other side, Poorna looked down at her body where the extremely hot water had hit her. The skin had reddened at a few softer places like her upper arms and her breasts. But now that she was out of the shower the water had started to make her feel cold while at the same time her skin demanded a distance from the hot water. She had heard the boy's question.

"Yeah, it's me."

"Are you okay?"

'Okay' wouldn't be even close to defining it. "No, I'm fine. I'm just a little burnt."

"Well, if you have Burnol you can use it and if not, you can just apply your toothpaste in the meantime."

"Thanks, but it's not that serious. It'll heal by itself."

"Where are you burnt exactly?"

"Well, most of it is on my hands and some of it on my boobs." *Shit!*

Silence.

"Um, I meant my chest."

"Yeah, that's okay. Just be careful with the hot water."

"Yeah, I thought I had set it right according to the timer, but I must've set the wrong heating setting."

"Just let it flow and after some time, it'll be less hot."

"Ok, I'll roger that. So what are we singing today?"

Shantanu was suddenly blank. He always had songs ready for the next three turns, but he couldn't remember what he had decided for today.

"Um, I'm thinking you should sing today."

Poorna sensed the tension in the sentence. She immediately understood that he was going through something. She thought of taking over out of sympathy.

"Ok, I'll sing today; but I won't give up my next turn." She tried to sound casual but even she knew that she had failed miserably.

"One minute." She said and walked back to the bedroom naked. The outside of the bathroom was colder and with her wet, naked body, she had shivering already and her teeth had started to chatter. She picked up the phone from the bed and went inside. She reached out for the soap-holder and replaced the soap with the phone. She turned the knob to the right to slow the shower stream down. She stood in the shower. Now it was the right kind of warm. The water still hurt a little in the places it had burnt her, but she needed the warmth.

She went on to YouTube and searched for a karaoke. She found the karaoke and played it. The song started with guitar sounds. As soon as he heard the guitar, he knew what song it was. It was a very popular song. He knew where he had to sing. Poorna cleared her throat a little bit and started to sing.

O re manwa tu toh baawra hai,

Tu hi jaane tu kya sochta hai,

Tu hi jaane tu kya sochta hai, baawre,

Kyn dikahye sapne tu sote jaagte?

Jo barse sapne boond-boond,

Naino ko moond-moond,

Hmmm, naino ko moond-moond,

Jo barse sapne boond-boond,

Naino ko moond-moond,

Kaise main chalu,

Dekh na saku,

Anjaane raaste.

Goonja sa hai koi iktara, iktara,

Goonja sa hai koi iktara,

Goonja sa hai koi iktara, iktara,

Goonja sa hai koi iktara,

Dheeme bole koi iktara, iktara,

Dheeme bole koi iktara,

Goonja sa hai koi iktara, iktara,

Goonja sa hai koi iktara.

The tune had started to play. Shantanu was standing in the shower with his head bowed, thinking about the way him and Chanda parted, maybe forever. He had ended his own potential love story. Couldn't he have gotten into a relationship with her and fallen in love with her later? Of course she was loveable. He could have fallen in love with her. Maybe he didn't try. While all such thoughts crossed his mind, one single thought answered all his questions. If he couldn't fall in love with her after knowing her all these years, how could he have fallen in love with her later? What would a relationship change between them? Nothing. It was as if he had started to write a story but didn't decide on its end.

All the while the tune was playing, Poorna was reflecting on the lyrics of the stanza she had just sung. The lyricist was right; the heart is actually a fool. With the enthusiasm she had while singing, nobody could've predicted that she was crying over her ex just a few minutes earlier. Now when she pictured her relationship with him, she could only remember flashes of the past, hurling at a speed that never made her feel anything. It was like keeping a time log of her relationship; just the track of activities happening, no feelings attached. Meanwhile, the end of the tune was near. Her 'singing reflex' readied her.

Sun rahi hoon sudh budh khoke,

Koi main kahani,

Poori kahani hai kya,

Kise hai pata,

Main toh kisiki hoke,

Yeh bhi na jaani,

Rut hai yeh do pal kiya,

Rahegi sada,

Kise hai pata,

Kise hai pata,

Kise hai pata,

Jo barse sapne boond-boond,

Naino ko moond-moond,

Hmmm, naino ko moond-moond,

Jo barse sapne boond-boond,

Naino ko moond-moond,

Kaise main chalu,

Dekh na saku,

Anjaane raaste.

Goonja sa hai koi iktara, iktara,

Goonja sa hai koi iktara,

Goonja sa hai koi iktara, iktara,

Goonja sa hai koi iktara,

Dheeme bole koi iktara, iktara,

Dheeme bole koi iktara,

Goonja sa hai koi iktara, iktara,

Goonja sa hai koi iktara.

As the song was ending with the piano sounds, so were their showers. Both of them didn't use soap. Shantanu didn't because he only had to rinse off his sweat. Poorna didn't because she was just too lazy to pick up the soap.

While drying themselves with towels, he asked her, "So how come you are bathing this late in the day?"

"I could ask you just about the same question."

"Well, I'm here because my underarms smelled and I hate that smell."

"What were you doing? Playing a game?"

He knew that she was just saying it for the sake of saying, but it held a different meaning for his conscience. *Maybe I* was *playing a game*, he thought. Snapping back to reality, he asked back, "Don't change the topic. Tell me your reason of bathing so late."

"I had a bunk today. So, I woke up late."

"What are you doing with your life?"

What did he say? "What the hell does that mean?"

"I mean that's your 9th bunk in two weeks; *and* we get the Sundays off. Aren't you worried you might lag behind?"

"No, I'm not worried."

"What about the pressure from your mother? Doesn't she want you to score good marks?"

"She's a bit old-fashioned. She believes that girls my age should be pleasing their husbands instead of entertaining ourselves with knowledge."

"What?"

"I'm sure she doesn't think like that. I'm just saying that my mother isn't entertained by the idea of a girl studying."

"So how come you're studying?"

"…Because of my father's wish."

"Your dad was the head of the house?"

"No, my grandfather is. It was my father's dying wish."

He didn't say anything further. He knew that he had crossed the line. He knew that Poorna was sensitive about her father. She, too, remembered the day she saw her father on his deathbed. It was like being teleported back in time.

Shantanu was about to apologize when he heard Poorna talking, "It was the 7th of February. The nature was in its full beauty. Our farms were yielding better than ever. But around the same time, my father had been advised bed rest by the doctor. The doctor had told us that nothing could be done in his case. They told us that he had reached the terminal stage of lung cancer. Doctor's calculation was that he only had a few days to live. When I, a child of age 13, asked him why this happened, he tried to tell me a religious story but I knew how things worked. So I asked him to tell me the truth.

He told me that the reason isn't known yet by science, but it could happen from anything. Their best guess was that it happened because my father unknowingly inhaled pollen consistently over the years with his works on the farms and his general presence near plants. The pollen that got stuck inside his bronchioles and the chemicals from the pollen caused the unnecessary proliferation of the cells. You know what 'bronchioles' and 'proliferation' means, right?"

"Yes; 'Bronchioles' are the site for exchange of gases in the lungs and 'proliferation' means growth or division." Shantanu, a biology student, replied almost instantaneously.

"Well, I didn't understand it immediately but the doctor told me not to tell my father everything right away. This breaks down the mental psyche of the patient. So we had told him when it was approximately 4 days since the diagnostic. We had hired a nurse but still my mother looked after him daily, taking time out from the farms.

When she told him what the doctor had told us, my father just called for me. As I entered the room, he asked everyone to go out.

Even with the IV strapped to his hand, he raised his hand and beckoned me closer. When I stood right beside his bed, he looked me in the eye. He said that he assumes that I know everything. I nodded. He slid a little to the left of the bed and asked me to join him. I slept beside him. I don't know why but the moment I felt his breath on my hair, I buried my face in his chest and started to cry. I didn't want him to go away. I could feel he had trouble breathing. His breathing was shallower than it used to be. I don't know how long I cried. He didn't even once stopped me, never told me not to cry or to stop crying. But then again, he never stopped me from doing anything.

I don't know how long I had cried when he asked me what the difference between a war and marriage is. I mustered up my words and told him I didn't know. He told me that the difference was that one could sleep with the enemy in a marriage. Even with the certainty of his death drowning me with tears, I laughed. Then he told me the only thing he said I needed to know in life. You know what he said?"

"What did he say?'

"He said, 'Poorna, as much as I've seen the world, I've always found it full of people overwhelmed with sadness and depression. The best I've learned from that world is this: Smile your best and you'll make it through your worst. Even tears make way for smiles.'"

"Then?" He asked after a full minute of silence.

"Then my father kept me hugging for some time. Then he called in my mother. He told her that I wouldn't be made to quit studies to help working on the farm. What I do after study is completely my decision. He also implied that I wouldn't ever be made to feel guilty in any way for my studies or anything that I do with my life. My mother, who had been a stubborn woman by nature, demanded that she needed some control over my life otherwise I'd ruin my life. There was some argument and then my father made amends. My mother would have a say in what I would study and that I would help on the farm whenever I'm home."

Shantanu and Poorna kept standing for a few minutes. Both of them didn't utter a word. The best type of condolence is silence, but it's also a dangerous one. One might just never know what to expect when a person is silent. She was the one to break the silence.

"That night, my father had a heart attack and the shock caused the lungs to seize. I was sleeping with my mother on the sofa right outside his room, just in case he calls for anything. But because his lungs were seized, he couldn't call for us loud enough. It was only after my mother went to check on him that we found out that he had died. The doctors had predicted the time of death to be 4:03 A.M., presuming that his heart attack and lung seizure cut off all the possible transportation of oxygen to his brain, causing his death faster."

"I'm sorry." It was all he could say.

"Nah, that's okay. It was and now feels like a long time ago."

"So?"

"What?"

"Do you smile often?"

XXXV

If it was any other day, any other person asking her, she would've easily lied. But there was something about that boy on the other side. It never felt okay about lying to him. She knew that he wouldn't be able to tell, but she didn't want to lie to him. After all, he was the only one she had shared about her father with. He had earned at least her truths.

"No, I don't, if I'm being honest. I smile usually as a general response to something nice, but since my father's death, I don't think I have ever smiled because of happiness."

"Do you know why?"

Poorna took a deep breath. He had asked a question that even she hadn't find the answer to. She swallowed once and exhaled.

"No. I don't know why I stopped smiling like that after my father. I do laugh every now and then, but I don't think I've ever smiled because of happiness."

"Never? Not even once?"

Poorna started to recollect the times she had happily smiled in life. It had been so less that she was able to count it now. Ever since she could remember, the first time she smiled happily was when she was introduced to the school books which had colorful illustrations along with great motivational stories. During her school life there were exactly 14 instances that she had smiled like that. Her fifteenth smile had been when her father took her to a tour of Golden Temple in Amritsar. The Golden Temple was a marvelous site to behold. Then up until her first period at age 13, her happy-smile count had reached up to 32. Then his father's lung cancer had happened, during that period, her smile had vanished. Her thirty-third smile had been on her father's deathbed. And ever since then, she hadn't smiled happily. But then something else struck her. It was the most recent instance of her smiling. Even she couldn't believe it. So the answer came out with a little uncertainty.

"The most recent instance of that is 5th December, 2018."

"What were you doing that day?"

He doesn't remember? "You don't know anything about 5th December?"

"Well, we don't exactly tell each other about our days here, do we?"

Poorna was a bit furious about him forgetting, but then the situation struck her. He thought that she smiled because of something happening later in the day. And when it happened they had a solid wall between them. He obviously couldn't know if she smiled that time or not. But being a girl, she wasn't going to give up the information that easily. So, she decided to play the game of hints.

"Well, let me give you a hint. It happened very early in the day, before the sun even rose."

He instantly understood what time she was talking about. A smile crept up on his face.

"So you're talking about *that* time?"

"Yes, I am."

"You're saying I made you smile?"

Somehow the happiness in that sentence made Poorna bow her head in shyness. It was almost as if he could see her from behind that wall.

"Yes, you did." She replied coyly.

"Well, I'm really happy to hear that."

On the other side, the way he meant each word of that sentence made Poorna feel like kissing him. Everything happened during that time flashed in her memories perfectly clearly. The song he sung, the way he sung it all night, the single hood celebration he prepared, his proposal in the song, everything.

She was feeling the same urge to confess that she had that same day. But she was still unsure of his feelings towards her. She was surprised at her own paradox. She could talk to him just about everything but she couldn't talk to him about her own feelings that she had started to have for him. She was somehow convinced that her proposal might complicate their already stable and happy 'relationship'. So, she again took a middle option. If he didn't understand, no harm done but if he did, then...

She had finished her toweling and wrapped her towel around her body and one on her head. As she was leaving, she yelled, "Hey!"

"What?"

"*I like your voice.*" She said and walked out the bathroom.

On the other side, Shantanu smiled shyly. He could feel the feeling in the sentence. But then he brushed it off with a shook of his head and walked out of the bathroom.

XXXVI

The alarm went off making an ear-piercing, shrill buzzer sound. It made Shantanu open his eyes with a jerk, as if a switch had been turned on. But the wide-eye awakening lasted only for half a second. After that, he started to tap around blindly looking for the phone. Once he got hold of the phone, he turned off the alarm and went back to sleep. When the alarm rang again, waking him up with a jerk, he looked at the alarm clock to find that only 10 minutes had passed. He hadn't turned off the alarm but had merely snooze it. This time he properly looked at the phone and turned off the alarm. Then he slumped back on the bed.

Then after the second alarm, which went off 20 minutes later, he finally pulled himself out of the bed. After turning the alarm off, he looked around and found that it was still dark out. He looked back at the bed. The outside was cold. As he touched the bed, it felt warm and inviting. 'Well, what's a little more sleep?' he thought and fell face first into the bed and slept.

The next time he woke up, it was 12:03 P.M. When he calculated, he found that he had slept six additional hours. Even though he had three hours to prepare, he decided to bunk the classes today. This would be his fourth bunk this month. He had woken up but he didn't have the energy to get up from the bed. It wasn't because he was unwell, but because he was feeling lazy. When he put his feet on the ground, he felt the cold surge upwards from his feet in an electric, slowly travelling chill across his body. He quickly wore slippers and started on his daily activities. After brushing, he felt the need for breakfast. But the thing about Shantanu was that he never ate without taking a bath. So, without delay, he went to his cupboard and took his towel and undergarments and went straight to the shower.

Inside the shower, he put his clothes on the bar beside him and waited for a sound. Then after waiting for five minutes in absolute silence, he sighed and said out loud, "Well, looks like she's not coming today." But the sound that hit his ears back wasn't just the reverberation of his voice; it was the voice of someone else's as well. He smiled on the acknowledgement and was about to ask her if that's her when he heard her asking, "Is that you?"

"Yes, it is me." he said smiling.

"You're late for your classes today."

"Well, I thought I should take a bunk today."

"Oh, god. What are you doing with your life?" She said mimicking him.

"Yes, yes, all right. What are we singing today?"

"Oh, about that. I got karaoke for that. I hope that you know this song."

"Well, let me guess. It's some famous bollywood song, right?"

"Yeah, right, good one."

The karaoke started to play. It started with guitar sounds. With a drop, it delved into a soulful melody. After another drop, Poorna started to sing.

Dhani si, dhani si,

Sharbat-e-paani si,

Dheere-dheere se teri chahat chadhti hai.

Thodi naadani si,

Thodi shaitaani si,

Dheere-dheere se teri aadat padti hai.

Tu hai to mere rubaru,

par kya karoon,

yakin hi nahi aata;

shaam se sawaal karoon,

dekha karoon,

raha bhi nahi jaata.

Afeemi, afeemi, afeemi hai yeh pyaar,

Afeemi hai tera mera pyaar,

Afeemi, afeemi, afeemi hai yeh pyaar,

Afeemi hai tera mera pyaar.

Khumaari, khumaari, naa aaye le karaar,

Afeemi hai tera mera pyaar.

Both of them were swaying to the tune while they were singing. He was happy with her choice of song. Otherwise, the songs were usually too fast and energetic for him. It wasn't that he couldn't keep up with them, but such songs hardly appealed to his moods. This song was one that settled both of their music tastes.

On the other side, Poorna was getting ready for the next stanza. She was hoping that he wouldn't disagree with what she had to propose after this song. She had picked out specifically that song for him. She knew he would like it better than all of her previous songs. She knew that it would put him in a good mood. Then she would ask him and there was a high chance that he would say yes. It's funny how human interactions are more of a work of wit rather than a cluster of emotions. As the stanza came, her 'singing reflex' signaled her, she was ready.

Thodi pighalti hoon,

Thodi phisalti hoon,

Gush kha ke teri hi Baahon mein girti hoon;

Thodi sarakti hai,

Thodi khisakti hai,

Neeyat bigad ke ye tujhse hi sambhle;

Tere-mere faasle,

Bas aaj se,

Sanson hi sanson mein gumne lage;

Tere-mere raaste,

Bas aaj se,

Aankhon hi aankhon mein milne lage;

Afeemi, afeemi, afeemi hai yeh pyaar,

Afeemi hai tera mera pyaar,

Afeemi, afeemi, afeemi hai yeh pyaar,

Afeemi hai tera mera pyaar,

Khumaari, khumaari, na aaye le karaar,

Afeemi hai tera mera pyaar,

The song ended with Poorna humming with the instrumental at the end of the song. Both of them were swaying at their positions as if they were performing a ballroom dance.

When Shantanu was drying himself, he heard sounds of throat-clearing from the other side. It wasn't because of a sore throat, it was obvious, but was a way of commanding attention. He smiled and said, "Yes?"

"Um, I wanted to ask you something."

"What is it?"

"Don't you think that we have been meeting in the showers for too long?"

He understood where this was headed. But to be true he didn't want to go there. He was already devastated with what happened with Chanda and what was going to happen with Chayansh. But for reasons unknown even to him, he couldn't just bring himself to say no. He stood silent for a while and then said, "I don't know how to answer that."

Poorna frowned on the other side. She expected deflection, maybe even a refusal, but she didn't expect a lack of response.

"It's a simple 'yes or no' question. There are no *ways* to answer that."

Shantanu fell silent. He wanted to get out of the shower that instant. He wanted to forget that this conversation ever happened. If he could control time, he would've gone back to the time the first alarm rang and wake himself up and get himself ready and send him to coaching and keep up this routine as long as he could avoid this conversation.

But he just stood there trying to form words like he was inventing them.

"I... I don't know. I mean... us, uh... we just... you know..."

On the other side, it was getting irritating for Poorna. She yelled out, "I'm *asking* you if we can finally meet. I want to see your bloody face. *There.* Now you're happy? Just answer the fucking question."

"Yes." He blurted out; then immediately regretted his answer.

"Okay, then. I don't know why you took so long to answer that question but since you agreed I have a function to attend this Sunday. We can meet there."

"Wouldn't it be weird and wrong to just show up like this?"

"Don't worry; I don't think anyone will notice. And in the case that there's a guest list, I'll put you up as my plus one. Okay?"

He sighed and said, "Yeah, alright."

"So you'll come?"

"Yes, I will."

"Okay, then, bye." Her voice sounded chirpy.

The sound of door closing on the other side echoed and Shantanu wrapped the towel around his waist but stood at his place contemplating the conversation he just had. A smile crept up on his face. He turned his head to look at the wall with the showerhead and whispered to it.

"It'll be a pleasure to meet you this Sunday, girl on the other side."

He let out a little laugh and smiled foolishly to himself. He got out of the shower and unwrapped his towel and started to dry his hair which still felt wet on their ends. While he was drying his hair, he was thinking about the time he would meet that girl: What he should wear, how should he talk to her, what would she look like, etc. When he tried to imagine her, suddenly Chanda's image popped up in his mind. He opened his eyes with nearly the same speed as the realization about Sunday hit him with.

He was due to meet Chanda and Chayansh this Sunday.

He was supposed to meet the girl on the other side this Sunday as well.

"Oh, this is not going to end well." He said to himself as he looked up and slowly pulled the towel off his face.

Forestory

Poorna had been sleeping in the bed, having dreams which made her smile. That was the time when her alarm went off. For the first fifteen seconds of blaring alarm, she didn't even stir an inch. After the dream finally had been broken, she grabbed her phone and opened her eyes squinting at the phone, partly in disgust and partly because the phone's screen was too bright. She turned off the alarm and turned in bed until she found a comfortable position and started to drift off. That was when she started to hear opera. It was some Italian lady singing in high pitch over prolonged duration of time. Her eyes opened that instant and with a renowned energy, she sat up on the bed and looked at the phone. The phone was still near the bed, its screen facing down. But she didn't have to look to know what was happening. She quickly pressed the 'lock screen' button on the phone's side and got out of bed and started to get dressed.

Poorna and Chanda had met first during her 9th class exams. Chanda's best friend Sonia had recently moved away and she was in need of some companionship. Poorna had always been the type of girl who doesn't say anything to anyone upfront but if meddled with, she could lash out with some of the greatest insults anyone ever heard. She also had an exception to this rule. Those she considered anything in her world she would never lash out on them.

She didn't expect a friendship from someone like Chanda. She used to think that friends with unequal financial statuses were only bollywood movie plotlines. But it somehow happened. She actually kicked it off really good with Chanda. They became best friends until the beginning of new session.

As the class 10th progressed, Poorna started to show the changes that told her best friend Chanda what puberty looks like. She became more self-aware as the puberty progressed and she started to notice the sexual hunger in people's eyes. So, one day, she proposed that they should have an emergency system so as to call each other when the one calling needs the other the most. Chanda readily agreed.

After brainstorming ideas and shooting down mountains of them, they both came to a conclusive system. In case of an emergency, they should send the distress signal by SMS texts since they are bounded only by network and SIM balance to deliver. To ensure that the message won't be ignored among other things, they both should set the messaging tones of each other with the type of sound they hate most. Poorna had chosen opera sounds because she didn't like the way it was sung. Chanda chose the song 'Axel F' of the character crazy frog because the 'ping, ping' sound irritated her. None of them had to use that system until now.

It was because of that same system that Poorna knew something was up. As soon as she finished dressing, she picked up the phone and checked what the message was. It read:-

'Come home. I need you. NOW.'

Even though the demand of coming home confused her, she decided not dwell on it too much and get to her house as quickly as she can.